The Kiss

of

Two Worlds

GW00724496

Alicen Geddes-Ward

Winged Feet Productions
Hemel Hempstead, Hertfordshire, England

The Kiss of Two Worlds
by
Alicen Geddes-Watd

A catalogue record for this book is available
from the British Library.
ISBN-978-0-9515329-2-8
ISBN-0-9515329-2-8

BIC subject category: FBC/HRDX9/VX

Cover production by Neil Geddes-Ward, Orkney, Scotland
Typeset in 10 point Times New Roman
Printed and bound by CPI Antony Rowe, Eastbourne
on recyclable, biodegradable paper
taken from sustainable sources

Alicen Geddes-Ward, together with her artist husband Neil, is also the author of the non-fiction book, Faeriecraft, treading the path of Faerie Magic (Hay House, London, 2005). As well as an author she is a Faerie Priestess and travels extensively throughout the UK giving workshops and lectures on faeriecraft. She is a regular columnist for many esoteric magazines internationally. Her numerous plays on faeries and esoteric themes have been performed worldwide. She has appeared on TV and is regularly asked to be a guest on radio programmes in the UK and US. She has been interviewed by many magazines and newspapers in the UK, US and Australia and has been described as 'the UK's leading exponent of faeries.'

With her husband she runs Orkney Faerie Museum & Gallery, Britain's only museum dedicated to faerie lore, based on the Orcadian island of Westray where they live with their two children.

www.orkneyfaeriemuseum.com

If you wish to contact Alicen or would like information on her other books, CD's, faerie workshops and forthcoming appearances, please write to:

Alicen Geddes-Ward
PO Box 1
Westray
Orkney
KW17 2WY

or email to alicen@geddesward.co.uk

Visit her websites at: www.faeriecraft.co.uk and www.faeriefellowship.com.
To see more of Neil Geddes-Ward's artwork visit www.neilgeddesward.com

Acknowledgements

It is never possible to write a book without the help and support of others.

I would like to thank my publishers for all their help and for taking the project on and my very helpful editors, Jill French and Chris Chibnall. Heartfelt thanks to Llewellyn and Juliana who always give me fantastic encouragement, when I need it most and believing in me.

Thank you to Bara for being the beautiful model in Neil's painting featured on the front cover and for Petr for his help and fun along the way.

Thank you to Drew and Be at www.Idobelieve.co.uk and Karen Kay of The Faery Ball for always believing and helping us all to keep the magic alive.

Loving thoughts to Neil and our children, Morgan and Tam Lin who will be relieved in the knowledge that they will have regular meals and clean clothes now this book is complete. To all my friends and family who have supported me over the years during the writing of this book.

Blessed Be to Queen Mab and all my faerie helpers who gave me this book.

Every effort has been made to contact the copyright holders of the quote in this book. The author was unable to contact Mabel Roxana Fernandez who sent the verse used in extract in the Epilogue. If she would like to make contact the author will be delighted to add an acknowledgment and rectify this in future editions of the book.

For Neil

Who never knew until it was too late that
'...there is nothing so difficult to marry as a novelist.'
(Peter Pan, the Movie, Columbia Pictures, 2004)

With Love
X

Also dedicated to the memory of W.B. Yeats and Maud Gonne
who gave the inspiration for this book.

The Kiss

of

Two Worlds

Alicen Geddes-Ward

Suspend your disbelief…

x

Contents

Prologue

The Indrinking Spell

'The queen of fairies she caught me
In yon green hill to dwell…
When fairy fold moun ride
And they that would their true love win …'

Anon, Tam Lin

The Faerie Rite; this is how it all began.

I remember the sweetest of scents on the night air as the Priestess of Elphame placed a bowl of honey on our faerie altar. The tree stump at the centre of our circle was covered in moss and decorated in chains of frothy hawthorn flowers. This was the night of Beltaine, the night when the veil to the Land of Elphame draws thin. It was a one-off, never to be repeated. We would enter a realm so entrancing, so captivating and all-consuming that we would never need to go there again. We knew that the faeries were the knowing within us, the secret places that we could not reach alone.

The Priestess of Elphame took up the besom and as she began to sweep the circle of the woodland floor, I gasped as I saw tiny blue sparks, like electricity, flying off the broomstick. "Spider, spider, what are you spinning? A cloak for a faerie, I'm just beginning," the Priestess sang as she swept and I could not keep my eyes from the broomstick that danced its sweeping way around our circle.

Once the circle had been prepared and cast, the Faerie Priest and I stood opposite one another. This was when I saw it: the beginning of the feeling that was never to end. We had both closed our eyes as he invoked the Faerie King, and the elfin magic that I shall never forget took us by the hands, drenching us in our star-spangled imaginations. I invoked the Faerie Queen Mab and it was then that we partook of the Indrinking Spell with one another. We entered Faerie Land, the place of

1

spiritual ecstasy and enrapture, where our existence and the place between-the-worlds kiss.

The Priestess of Elphame placed a crown of hawthorn flowers upon our heads and kissed us in turn. My Faerie Priest and I leant forward and we kissed the kiss of no return. For, as if it was the trigger of a gun, on the moment of the kiss, I felt hit by a physical blow. It was something full of radiance that entered me at lightening speed, as if it was a thunderbolt tearing out of the heavens, with me the unwitting target. My heart had been laid bare by a careless husband and now, within a circle of candles it had been taken, in an instant, by someone else. I was stunned and reeled in confusion. From that night on we became the King and Queen of Cobwebs within the Faerie Ring of Queen Mab, where on that Beltaine night, we invoked the freedom to begin a journey which opened us to the place where our bodies are not forbidden in the secret place between the worlds.

From then I knew that faeriecraft is an art. It would not judge, but would let me experience the extreme and deliver its verdict through an intense, emotional encounter. Feeling desire like a religion our wraith bodies began the journey to know one another's souls like fingerprints.

This is the seeding of my story where I await on the elven altar of my imagination for the kiss of two worlds.

Follow me if you will…

Chapter One

The Remembering

*'Entering the time not of men, the faerie queen
blinks her sea-green, slanted elven eyes and
gently extends her hand.
Take her hand.*

It is now that the journey begins.'

The Faerie Mound

I want you to imagine a woman: I want you to close your eyes and see her, see her whole being, for through these pages and beyond, she can be yours. If you can believe in the place between the worlds… now touch her, smell her, taste her.

I had looked at myself in the mirror, as if it was my lover as I stood naked before the moonlit glass, my clothes strewn about me. You must keep me as secret and as silent as a séance. For magic is only in the unspoken and the unseen. Walk with me through these pages and I will tell you about the intoxication of real faerie magic.

Last summer, quite by accident, I felt that I had overdosed on life. At the same time I feared my true sexuality was buried with the rest of my nine to five existence. I knew about the gaps in time, where art, sex and inspiration lived. I knew if my dreams grew desperate enough I could send out a thought to find someone to unearth my sexuality, my self, my secret dangerous self.

WANTED: Archaeologist with clean fingernails and kisses that contain words to fill me.

I parcelled up my secret thoughts in brown paper and hairy string and posted them in an ethereal scarlet post box, clearly marked *Thoughts are Things*. Lying to myself was a favourite hobby, for I already knew who my archaeologist was and I had wanted him, even before I had realised it. I had tried not to want him; why should I have him when I already have someone else? Isn't that greedy- wanting two lovers?

The thought had sometimes crossed my mind, to have three.

It began last summer, after I had realised that my secret thoughts were growing more engulfing, each time I saw him. He had opened a door within me that had revealed my hidden self, the self I didn't really want to admit to. It was a part of me that had, until then, remained in shadow. Now I gazed into the mirror at my other self in all her darkness, I wasn't sure that I liked her. I may not have liked her, but I wanted her and once the darksome longing door had been opened, I couldn't help myself.

On an early May evening, I had sat by my open bedroom window and watched; for how long, I really cannot remember, the day air filling with night. I had been trying to fool myself that only my body thought of him. I knew it was impossible for us to become entwined, as my husband trusted me, and my archaeologist had a girlfriend somewhere. I had never met her; perhaps that's what made it easier on my conscience.

It had been time to go, and as I pulled on my comfortable, worn-out jeans and T-shirt, and slipped on my sparkly sandals. I had thought, *the trouble is, not even my body should be thinking of him,* as I closed the front door behind me. Now follow me to my place, where real life is suspended for a while. Where is your place, where you hang real life up in a wardrobe and put your escapist clothes on? I want to tell you about my place; if you've ever been there you'd know. It's a place where reality stops and the gap between time begins. Most people go there by accident once or maybe twice in a lifetime, or in their night dreams. I go there on purpose whenever I can.

I had made my way to the meeting place that evening, along the pathway in Chesham Bois where I lived. My skin had felt smooth and light as I had bathed only an hour before. The air seemed alive with happenings to come, as was my imagination, I could almost see the magic about me in the dusky light in the walk up to the Wharton's house. It was only a fifteen minutes brisk walk, along a tree-lined footpath. The trees whispered words to me as I made my way hurriedly to the meeting. Their secret, swishing language clung to my heightened imagination, as the words caught the breeze. As I approached Kel and Katri's suburban road, I sighted their well kept Victorian terraced house, which was situated opposite the pleasant village green. The streetlights dropped pools of fuzzy amber light onto the pavement in the dusk. As I walked underneath a streetlight, I checked my watch; I was a little late, but it would not matter.

As I walked up the Wharton's pathway, their pristine black front door was slightly ajar, an open invitation. If only everyone knew that the door was always open. As I entered the meeting, I immediately felt, as I knew I would, a sense of relief and a belonging, that I was among company that would accept me. The world looked upon the others in the meeting, as strangely as they looked upon me.

"Hi Jessa, we're just about to begin. If you want a drink, it's in the fridge. Can you get me one while you're there?" Kel kissed me and handed me his empty glass, I smiled at his cheek and went to the kitchen where I found Ned sitting on the work surface, his legs dangling.

"I've been waiting for you," he said, jumping from the worktop that was strewn with dirty dishes, coffee mugs and leftovers from dinner.

"Oh yes." I answered, opening the fridge door, taking out a bottle of white wine. "Do you have a glass behind you?"

"It depends if you want a clean one or not." He half-heartedly sorted through some glasses on the work surface. "How about this one?" he said passing me a pint glass with cigarette ash in it. He grinned as I handed it back to him.

"Try again," I said, as he passed me a coffee mug, containing cold coffee. "Are we going to play this game all evening?" He took the coffee mug from my hands and gave me a clean wine glass. Then he took the bottle of wine from me and poured it out.

"Would you like to taste the wine Madam?" he asked, passing me the wine.

"I'll take your word for it." I took a gulp and he put the bottle back in the fridge.

"So?"

"So what?" he said, jumping back on the work surface, fiddling with the silver rings on his fingers.

"So why have you been waiting for me?"

"Kel wants the Ring to go to the woods after the meeting. We know it's short notice, but will you come? We haven't worked a ritual for ages because Katri's been away. Kel just wants to get together and do something creative." I contemplated my husband-quandary. Michael wasn't around very often, he lived in the real world. He had a real job and he liked being a grown-up, unlike me. Michael trusted me, and I him, however he did not know that I did not trust myself. Trust is a dangerous thing between lovers, it slips out of your hands, when you are least expecting it, when you didn't want it to go. Then you are left in the place that guilt lives.

But sometimes danger can be a pleasure.

"All right I'll come," I replied "what's Kel drinking?"

"Guinness, I suppose. Here give me his glass and I'll take it out. We're sitting in the garden and we're just about to begin; we'd better go through." Ned took the glass and we left the cluttered kitchen. We entered the meeting, my place, the place where I belong.

As I walked into the Victorian walled garden, I saw my archaeologist sitting under the apple tree on a pile of cushions. He was smoking a cigarette and holding a bottle of ale; always poised, but his cigarette, laced with the more deluding and exciting concoction, would always reach his lips first.

Suddenly someone placed their cool hands over my eyes from behind. "Guess who?" said a warm female Scandinavian voice. I immediately gasped in excitement and grabbed her slender hands.

"Katri!" I turned around to face my Priestess of Elphame, the co-leader of the Faerie Ring group; we hugged tightly and kissed each other on both cheeks. I adored Katri and she always seemed to have a mothering thing with me. She was the editor of a national esoteric magazine and she was also style personified. She always wore a scarf somewhere; either tied around her neck, head or through the waist of her vintage faded jeans. She was slim and possessed poise, grace, intelligence and beauty all framed by her sleek black long hair and sparked with her Finnish blue eyes. "How come you're home so soon, is everything okay?"

"Yeah I'm great actually. I had to come home a little early to sort out some work stuff at the magazine. So...here I am!"

"Kel must be relieved; I thought he was reverting back to bachelordom."

"You noticed too! Housework was never his strong point." She pushed her dark hair out of her eyes and looked a little more intently at me. "And how about the Faerie Ring?" "We've been meeting weekly, but it's just been Ned's soup and chat, no rituals, which has been fine, but not quite the same without you. Well we're going to make up for lost time and have a ritual tonight – game?"

"Can't wait."

Kelsey came over to us and kissed me. He was warm-hearted and dependable, tall, black-bearded and faintly handsome. A graphic designer who worked from home, he completed the firm and loving twosome who had founded the Faerie Ring of Queen Mab. "Can you stay late for a Faerie Circle Jessa, we're just itching to get the Ring back together again now that Kat is home?"

"That'll be great."

"We thought at about nine, when we've got all the chat out of the way, we'll all take a walk to the woods. It will be our first ritual since Laurie and you were made King and Queen of Cobwebs." Laurie and I had taken on these roles; the deputies to Katri and Kelsey who were the Priest and Priestess of Elphame and also considered to be the physical embodiments of the King and Queen of Faerie within a ritual setting. The symbolism of the cobweb was the echo of the spiral in the shape of the spider's web, the spiral being a universal portal to the Land of Faerie and the Otherworlds. Laurie and I were now the keepers of that magical doorway and entry to those realms was our purpose.

Ned broke into the conversation; "Are you going to tell her Katri?" "Tell me what?" I asked intrigued. Katri grinned and turned to Ned. "Ned can't wait because it's all his doing you see."

"Put me out of my misery won't you?"

"Remember I said ages ago that the next new member of the Ring will be your apprentice? As you know, Ned is working with Kelsey and I'm too tied up caring for Dylan to take on someone at the moment. So it's all down to you!" explained Katri. "She should be here at the end of the meeting, so we can introduce her to you. We think she'll be perfect because she needs someone sensitive to guide her", said Kel.

"He means that she's the sort of person we're going to have to scrape off the ceiling after every meditation, she's that psychic," interjected Ned. "She's on my course at Uni, but she's younger than me, twenty one I think."

"Velvet's very fey, she's going to make a gifted Faerie Priestess," said Katri.

"And that's where I come in. Velvet you said?"

"Her parents are actors," answered Ned. "I don't think she wants to follow in their footsteps though. She's kind of shy and academic."

Kel broke in, "Lets get on with it then, we've got loads to catch up on now that Kat's back. It's elven time, let's start shall we?" He gestured for everyone to sit on the rugs under the apple tree boughs. The fresh scent of the apple blossom caught my senses as we made ourselves comfortable. As Kelsey leant against the trunk of the apple tree, Katri reclined on her back and rested her head on Kel's outstretched thighs. The garden looked magical in the fading light, as Katri had placed candles in glass containers in the garden; some hanging from the branches of the tree and others at the base of the trunk, infusing a golden hue to our Faerie Ring gathering. Laurie stayed where he was; the silent observer as always, and Ned sat cross-legged next to me.

The part of myself that I didn't trust and the part that I didn't really know, wanted Laurie, and that made me feel dangerous to myself. These feelings had come from nowhere, they had sparked within when he had first smiled at me. I had stupidly ignored those feelings, snaking throughout me, making sure that every part of me felt something for him. I was brimming with feelings for him. They were the sort of feelings, that if you put them all in a box and shut the lid on them, they'd pop open the lid. Every time you pushed those beautiful, glittering snakes back in their box and closed the lid, it would pop open again and again. They were out of control inside me, as if feelings for him were spiralling their way through all my organs and my mind, clogging my usual thoughts. I wasn't going to let anyone know about my secret.

Not even him.

My trouble was what could I do with my box of writhing snakes? They were not happy in a box, they wanted to be set free. If I tell someone about this, it will become a real happening and guilt will overcome me. There are some things that are broken if one speaks of them.

You're doing it again and you don't even know you're watching him do you?

I scolded myself as I turned my back on his smiling eyes. I could get away from his stare, but I could not escape the garden's atmosphere. It was the spirit of the place that touched me, for it had a quality of sensuality. Everywhere was sexuality, it clung to people's words, it created auras around their bodies and spiralled around the space, like the incense smoke, that was whirling this way and that. Was I the only one that felt it, was I the only one, who secretly loved another, or did everyone else live on secret thoughts too?

I had momentarily closed my eyes and leant right back on the rug, taking in the mood of the garden. I allowed my senses to be filled with the smells all around me, of incense smoke, wine, and scented candles. This was my place, where people became what was unreal to others- that doesn't even exist for others, who tread the nine-to-five existence of conformity. Here was aliveness among these secret sharers of magic and all I had ever wanted to do, was to drown in it and never surface again.

I began to lose the thread of Kel's words and his voice started to feel hypnotic and dream-like. The scent of the apple blossom took on a strange, tangible quality as if I was riding upon it and I could feel it carrying me somewhere; to a destination unknown: I was so immersed in the encounter that I cared not where I was heading. I began to feel as if I was floating. Although my eyes were shut, the garden vision was clear to me through another seeing, I saw the gnarled trunk of the apple tree glisten and shimmer, as if inviting me. As I watched the glimmering tree, a little knobbly wooden door slowly made itself visible to me in the base of the trunk. It was as if the door was always there; only I did not ordinarily have the sight to perceive it. I began to see a golden cord attached to my body and ascend to the heavens, and all at once, like a rush of realization, I felt my connectedness with the universe and the god/goddess energy. I experienced myself to be a spiritual being within a human body and I could see this spiritual being flashing inside my body with a transfixing electric-blue light. I began to feel as if this is what it must be like when you are about to die; on the precipice of this world and the next, experiencing the window to heaven being open and fluid. I knew that I was seeing beyond the real and feeling like an eternal being.

Then, as if it couldn't get any weirder, my own voice began speaking to me as if my all-knowing soul self was speaking. This is the Remembering, my own voice said to myself inside my head, but from where it came I know not. As if these words were the key to open the apple tree door, my spiritual body shot forward and entered through the little door to where I was coming to understand that I was about to arrive full circle at the star explosion of realization. The bewilderment of it all was beginning to make strange, but crystal clear sense, as I journeyed through the door. I must have shrunk in size, Alice-In-Wonderland style as I entered to find, not the inside of a tree trunk, but a different realm entirely.

Under the earth and away from man, is a forgotten secret, well-hidden and silent. It has been buried for centuries and all but unremembered. Once upon a time man used to share the secret and live by it and also live side-by-side with the silent people, known to us as the faeries. You know the story only too well, for man grew arrogant and thought that he was smarter than the secret; thought that he had outgrown it and so he discarded the knowledge until all that was left of it was buried beneath the cairns and crumbling skeletons of the ones who once knew.

I journeyed beneath the Earth to the place of the shrouded knowledge. All around me was dusky light, as if the sun was just setting over the horizon. Here all of nature was magnified, as if to look at each flower would plunge me through a portal to another world and parallel dimension. The scene I beheld was an orchard in a lush meadow, bespeckled with buttercups, oxeye daisies and swaying grasses. The beauty was so overwhelming that my senses were almost overloaded. In the golden light I saw a man and a woman and when I set eyes upon them I knew that I had come home. This was indeed *the Remembering* and this was where I hailed from. I knew them to be the King and Queen of all Faerie and these were my kin. All at once it was as if I had never been away and the Jessamyn life that I had just journeyed from, felt like a dream that I could forget if I wished. This remembrance I knew was the real life and Jessamyn was just a voyage to excavate the hidden knowing, not just for me, but for everyone who wished once again to know the secret.

The Faerie King and Queen in their sparkling, resplendent garb, held out their hands and I instinctively put out my hand which they held warmly and lovingly. No words were spoken, as all feeling was in the knowing silence and I knew that this was a glimpse at my eternal existence beyond the veil. I felt swathed in the god/goddess love and surrounded by invisible angelic beings, and everything was goodness intensified, as if I had entered heaven.

I felt my own body calling me, as if the hand was without its glove. The Faerie King and Queen both kissed me upon the cheeks and I felt as if I was being kissed by angels, so divine was their touch. I released my hand from theirs and in a sudden spiral of upward swirling movement, I found myself outside the apple tree door and heading towards my waiting body, which lay in a peaceful repose on the rug among my Faerie Ring friends. I melded surprisingly effortlessly into my body and

I could hear Kelsey and Katri chatting, but it was as if they were a long way off.

I felt as if I had been shocked back into my body with the realization that I had experienced a spiritual epiphany of unknown depth and weirdness, of which I was yet to unravel.

Ned had tapped me lightly on the hand and I opened my eyes, quite suddenly, a little startled. I realised that everyone in the garden was quiet now. I felt dazed at the experience I had just encountered and unable to join in properly with the meeting. Katri started to get everyone more drinks and prepare for Velvet's arrival. I could only feel his stare burning into the back of my head, and he wanted me, I knew that. It made me scared that someone may have read my thoughts, my thoughts that were so loud inside my head, that I felt I may have spoken them aloud in the garden. At one moment I had to look over my shoulder at him, I could not help it. I was right, for he was staring entirely into my being. His dark eyes asked questions when he looked at me and I answered them with thoughts that I did not want to reach him. I had to quickly turn back, turn away from his want of me, as he was pulling my heart towards him, as if it were on a thread. The longer I stayed at the meeting, the less I thought of my Michael. The less I thought of my other life and the more I became immersed in their words. Time was away and somewhere else and I was engulfed within an indrinking spell of thoughts and feelings.

The Faerie Ring was a collection of five (soon to be six) like-minded people. We came together to practice the spiritual pathway of faeriecraft; the creative melding of the faerie faith and natural witchcraft. Yes, we all believed in faeries and lived our lives by the ancient principles of faeriecraft. The way I felt in their company was mostly indescribable. They had all come together to share the hidden places in themselves. Freedom of the self is a very strange thing. It makes people behave differently to when they are among 'polite society'. People who are free in themselves wear aliveness in their eyes and their sexuality is almost visible. It is as if their sexuality has seeped to the surface of their skin and it is glistening all over their bodies. As if they have dipped a brush in a pot of glitter marked 'sexual aliveness' and painted it all over themselves. Now imagine being in a garden with five people, who all had pots of that glitter painted on their flesh. Can you but wonder why I was so transfixed with the company I kept that night?

I must have still been away with the faeries because my archaeologist, Laurie, had quite silently seated himself, cross-legged on the rug next to me, whilst everyone else in the garden was talking amongst themselves. "I can't think of anything better," he said taking a swig from his bottle of ale.

"I'm sorry?" I answered, thinking how stupid he must think me.

"A summer rite, knee deep in mud in the middle of some woods. Kel's quest for creativity?"

"Oh yes of course. I was in a world of my own just then."

"Meditating?" he asked smiling, his eyelids appearing laden with alcohol and night as he spoke to me. "I suppose that sounds a better excuse than just not listening."

"Are you going?"

"I've said I will, but it really comes down to how the land lies at home. It's difficult to get away sometimes and I get fed up with all the explaining. Do you have that too?" He offered his bottle of beer to me and I took some. My hands were shaking slightly as I passed it back to him and he looked into my eyes to ask why, but I averted my gaze for a moment, feeling self-conscious. I could not tolerate his asking eyes. "Not really, she doesn't understand, but she doesn't ask either. In fact to tell you the truth, she doesn't know anything about this. I prefer to leave it at that, it's simpler in the long run." He ran his fore finger absent-mindedly up and down the surface of his brown ale bottle and gazed at the others in the garden for a moment.

As he did so I watched him closely, his skin flushed with alcohol and sensitivity. I watched him at every opportunity, when I thought that I would not be noticed, secretly studying his person. His skin was also alive with his sexuality and it reminded me of the complexion of some elfin creature, whose skin reflected the fecundity of nature. If I reached out, I could have lightly touched his face, and if I had done so, there would have been no doubt that he would have welcomed my touch. However, I always had Michael at the back of my mind. *Only my body thinks of him,* I had said to myself, as the attraction towards him became dangerous within me.

Kel was beckoning to Laurie on the other side of the garden. He passed me his beer bottle and standing up said; "I won't be a minute." He left me in a pool of his presence, feeling infused by his personality. The Wharton's fox coloured cat, with her knowing eyes, sidled up to me, rubbing her neck and ears around my knees, purring as she did so.

She basked in the company of all the strangers, walking seductively from one visitor to the next, taking a stroke from each, making sure that she visited everyone. Now it was my turn. I put down Laurie's beer bottle and began caressing Bella's head as she pushed against me fondly. Bella was a passionate feline and in her purring, distracted state, she momentarily forgot herself and knocked over the bottle of beer. With a start she ran, tail between her legs, her ears down, out of the garden and into the house. I however, had been left in a puddle of beer, which was quickly soaking my jeans. With a bump, I had been brought back to earth.

Taking the almost empty bottle with me, I hurriedly made my way into the house and up the steep stairs into the Wharton's bathroom. I locked the door behind me and sat down on the bathroom scales, plunging my face into my cupped hands. I sat contemplating my sticky situation for a moment. I was a dress size smaller than Katri, so there would be nothing I could borrow and I was beer-soaked through to my knickers, the only solution would be to go home and come back later to the ritual. I just wanted to slip away, unnoticed into the anonymous night air. There was an impatient knock at the bathroom door. "Will you be long?" asked a Ned sounding voice. I opened the door and stood face to face with Ned, who grinned when he realised it was me. "Well?" "Well what?" I answered. "Will you be long; I'm starting a queue here." "Come in for a minute," I said taking his hand and coaxing him into the bathroom.

"What do you mean Jessa?" he asked suggestively and we both laughed as I locked the door behind us to avoid anyone else seeing my predicament.

I pointed to the large soaked patch on the bottom of my jeans. "It'll dry," he said grinning.

"It reeks, I've got to go home and get changed."

"That'll take ages, Velvet has just arrived, and that's why I came to find you and what about the ritual in the woods afterwards? Kel really wants you there, you've told him you're going to come already." Ned sat down on the toilet seat lid, took a cigarette from his shirt pocket and lit up. "I had come in here for a reason, I'm bursting actually, that beer went through me really quickly."

"I'll leave you to it. Perhaps I'll go out the back door." Ned caught my arm softly as I was undoing the lock on the door.

"You can't go home; you said you'd be there."

"Okay, I'll go down and meet Velvet now, but then I'll go home to get changed. I'll go straight to the woods afterwards, it won't take me long."

"On your own?" he asked with a look of concern. "I'll be all right, I've got a torch."

As I entered the heavily scented garden I saw a young girl who must have been Velvet and she certainly lived up to her sensual name. The garden was now in complete darkness and was lit by the flickering candles hanging in the branches of the apple tree and standing on the rug. It was an enchanting sight and Velvet did not look out of place. The moment I saw her, I knew we were going to have fun together. She was very slightly built with long honey blonde hair framing an oval fey featured face with cat like brown eyes. She grinned when she saw me entering the garden and Katri turned and smiled too.

"We were wondering where you were, did Ned find you?" asked Katri.

"He did, along with my sticky situation," I pointed at my beer soaked jeans. "I'll have to nip home and get changed soon, if I'm going to make it back in time for the 'Rite."

"How did that happen?"

"Bella."

"That would explain her mad dash into the house. Oh sorry," she turned to Velvet. "This is Velvet and she's dying to come to the ritual, but of course it's a little early for that yet. I've told her that she will work with you for a while, perhaps you can fix a date to meet up, I know Velvet's keen to get started?"

"Hi, pleased to meet you," I said and shook Velvet's delicate hand and I almost felt that I had touched a faerie. "And what draws you to work with the fey?"

"It's not so much me that wants to work with them, but the other way around."

"Oh?" I asked.

"They've always been in my life, since I was a child and I have always loved them, but kept it to myself of course; Lately though, they keep hiding objects and I find them in odd places and my dreams are just…weird, all of a sudden. I do just dream about faeries and a message all the time, in fact it's driving me a bit insane and I thought if I tried to explore what they want, they might get off my case. And then I met Ned and we got talking and here I am."

"I've got a feeling this is going to be interesting, when would you like to meet then?"

"Well, I'm free tomorrow after my tutorial around six o'clock, is that too soon?"

"That would be great. Why don't you ring me at work tomorrow and I'll give you directions to my house. I work at the town library. Just ask for Jessamyn Fawn and I'll see you tomorrow then."

"Okay, I'll do that." She grinned broadly and I turned and headed towards the garden gate. As I did so I caught Laurie's eye and he shot me a look so intense, it nearly stopped me dead in my tracks.

"See you later," he said as if it was an invitation and I managed to smile and hurried away.

The heavy dark air enwrapped me as I walked through the floral scented garden to the tall, black wrought iron gate and as I closed it, I left that potent gathering of friends behind me. I felt the real world touch me sharply as the gate clanged shut and I hurried along the street, feeling alone in my wordiness of secret thoughts for another, and entranced by their threading through my mind.

* * *

Can you see me?

Concentrate on the blackness now, penetrate its wholeness and push the little lights away from your eyes. Yes, now you see me in the darkness that is so very alive and tell me, tell me; what do you see?

Jessamyn Fawn lying naked on the duvet.

See my body and imagine running your fingertips, only your finger tips mind you, over the velvety skin. Imagine your body next to mine.

You can't? Why is that so? Because there is already someone else lying next to me.

A few moments after I had arrived home, I had just taken my jeans off and Michael must have noticed that my clothes and my hair smelt of incense smoke. "Where have you been?" he had asked, looking tired as he poured me a glass of white wine to match his own. I explained in the usual censored terms of the meeting. I dare not tell him that I was only home to change my clothes. "I don't remember you telling me anything about a meeting. Never mind now, I've had a long day and I've missed you," he kissed me on the lips and then taking my hand, led me upstairs to our bedroom. We did not switch the light on, for it would have shown what our faces were feeling.

From then on I experienced no perception of passing time. Our togetherness like this had been long awaited, for his work had kept him from me and my secret thoughts had stopped me wanting him so much: until these moments. Our limbs entwined and our arms encircled and it felt good to be held again. We plunged into the wanting of one another and I forgot the evening and where else I was supposed to be, for to be kissed in every secret place was delicious enough to fill all my senses. I felt totally immersed in the business of wanting him, as we fell giggling and naked onto the bed.

He lay on top of me, kissing my neck so lovingly.

"You really have missed me then?"

"Of course, Jessa."

"And I have missed you … a bit." I teased, pushing him off me playfully, giggling and moving to change position, so that I would be the one on top of him. He fell willingly beneath me and as he did so I gasped out loud, shocking even myself with my reaction and for a moment I was unable to think what I should do. For instead of Michael lying beneath me… I saw Laurie, lying beautifully naked and smiling up at me. He appeared in Michael's place as if a flash of lightning had thrown him there. It was all so overwhelming, that I swear I could count every freckle upon his face and I could take in every detail of his bare skin. He appeared real, vital and immediate and he was not motionless, as if he was superimposed over Michael. No, he smiled up at me, as if he knew that he was appearing before me and his eyes twinkled. I felt giddy, confused and overcome and then before I could really contemplate the bizarre situation, he vanished in the same phantasmic instant that he had appeared.

Michael was looking up at me puzzled, as I sat astride him. "What's the matter?" he quizzed me and I had to think in a split second to cover myself.

"It's okay; I just twisted my ankle slightly when I turned over." I began to kiss him intensely on his neck to distract him. "It was nothing; it's alright now, just one of those things when you get a sharp pain and then it's gone." The moment thankfully diffused itself, but from then on only my body was with Michael and my first thought was; *shit, I'm in trouble, I'm in deep trouble.* My thoughts went back to Beltaine night when I had received a similar sensation when Laurie had kissed me and my world had shifted in a flash. I now knew what that physical thing had been, the thunderbolt that had hit me as if out of the blue; I was in love with Laurie. I had always heard about the love that hits you so hard it is like Cupid's arrow penetrating you, but I had always assumed that it did not really exist, for with Michael I had gently slipped into love, almost willingly. This was like being held love hostage at arrow point and I knew exactly what had happened. My heart had been neglected and was breaking, Laurie was the one who had begun to mend it and here was Michael, just a little too late to see to the damage. Now it wouldn't do, things were going to get messy, I could see that.

Was it some kind of hallucination or had Laurie's astral body actually appeared to me? Could he have sent me a phantom of himself? I had never encountered such an engaging and stunningly disturbing experience. Was I mad, or was this a message from my psyche or even Laurie himself? The very fact that he had taken the place of my husband chilled me and I knew that Laurie had stolen me to a secret place where I was experiencing life once removed, yet magnified.

From then on I just went through the motions of making love. I made noises in all the right places, but Michael felt like a stranger. I felt withdrawn and the only thing that kept my attention were the confused, shocked words inside my head.

Mine are the words that are not enough, that feel, but they never get deep, they only scratch the surface. You have to fill in the blanks. His brown eyes looked into mine and I smiled. There was a deep silence inside my head and thoughts behind my face that could never be words.

But words are what I am for you now. So see me now, Jessamyn Fawn lying naked on the duvet, wearing my just-loved, just-kissed face, watching the dark room and feeling its heaviness. I lie not by myself, but alone, in the weighted darkness that hangs all around me and the full-length mirror that stood on the far side of the room beckons. Could I still make it in time for the ritual? I wondered as I peered at the face of my sleeping husband? I felt comforted to be near him, in his arms that knew and understood a reality that I could not be part of.

I glanced over to the big chrome alarm clock, its hands illuminated in the dark. *Half past ten.* I thought to myself that I still may have time to reach the Faerie Ring woodland gathering, even if the magic-making was over, I could explain the circumstances that had kept me from arriving in time. The sloping floorboards had creaked as I stepped out of bed, but my contented sleeper did not stir. I could not even hear his breathing, let alone his dreamful thoughts. My thoughts were already in another place, with another one.

As I washed my husband from myself, alone in the bathroom, dangerous words danced and weaved within me. My hands washed the love from my womanly body and I felt acutely to be a little girl, who had grown up quite by accident.

I felt very excited at the prospect of stealing out into the night, unnoticed by my slumbering man. It felt like something a heroine would do in an 18th century novel. My woodland destination held promises as I readied myself. I felt exhilarated and deep in thought, entranced by the idea of meeting my beloved Faerie Ring and especially with meeting Laurie. Sometimes I dared not even think his name for the feelings that it evoked within me.

I had pulled on my velvet dress and cloak and I turned to face the bed. Michael had turned over, his eyes still closed and had placed his hand on my empty pillow, where I had been so guiltily a few moments before. Guilty of thinking wrongs that were so much part of myself. He snuffled dreamily, as if he were a little boy again, then he rolled over and opened out his tight body and I remembered that he was a man. Assured that he was sleeping soundly, I stole out of the loving room and out of our togetherness house. I prayed that he would not awake to see my absence as the night enfolded me into its atmosphere.

I am occasionally afraid of the dark. *Was I afraid of the darkness within? Is the raven black night simply a reflection of the darksome river that ran through me, that I had never yet had the courage to drink?* As I made my way hastily to the alluring woods, I felt all of reality to be around and about me, but not within me as usual. Outside of myself, I saw the night swathed streets and the occasional car drive past me. I felt that they were all real and belonged in the tangible world and I - did not.

I inhabited a place more distant, a place which did not connect up with the touchable. Perhaps I was experiencing a faulty connection. Unfortunately I know of no astral electricians in the Yellow Pages. I secretly thought that I may be slightly mad. Madness is a positive asset if you are an artist. What a pity I was only a librarian.

I searched for the copse, where I knew the Magic Place to be. The trees seemed to confuse me and all I could perceive for a few moments was the penetrating darkness and the searching, rushing, speaking wind. I wrapped my cloak about me and tried to get my bearings, but all around me was unrecognisable. Suddenly from behind me I heard the snap of a twig underfoot; I turned around and gasped, only to face Kelsey smiling. "It's only me, we saw you turn the wrong way, follow me," he turned and led the way through some thick undergrowth, to where I suddenly saw the others, surrounded by a circle of torch candles staked in the earth. It was a magical sight, as if I had stumbled upon a secret faerie grotto that could only be glimpsed for a second. I wondered then, why I had not seen the lights in the copse in the beginning; it seemed so obvious now. Laurie and Ned were waiting for me, both in their beautiful velvet robes and Katri stood by the altar in her mediaeval style dress and crushed velvet midnight blue cloak. Kel handed me a drink of wine in a wooden chalice and I gladly drank it to feel that the attention was not solely upon me.

Now standing in the woods, chalice of wine in hand; I was a Faerie Priestess with the Ring, about to enter the spider's web entrance to Faerie Land; to catch my own dreams as well as someone else's.

Chapter Two

The Magic Place

'Begin ...
... the weird, weird of weirdness.'

We five faerie seekers wore the full moon in our eyes and did not demand words from one another. Words were now untouchable within our circle of knowing, as we all chanted our faerie verse to bring out the secrets within ourselves. Our chants spiralled around the black trees and through our veins, tingling the skin and freeing our thoughts.

We stood, encircled within our invoked magic, hands clasped, like knots of flesh, to form a wheel of intensity. Vitality prickled over my skin as we all began to tread a spiral, walking in a circular motion, all the while following a spiral pattern in our mind, until we reached the centre of our self-made spiral; the symbolic doorway to the Land of Faerie. Katri suddenly broke the circle and took my hand, drawing me to the centre, where a small, black old cauldron was placed. She knelt down and swished her hands rapidly in the vessel of water and I sat down next to her on the earthy woodland floor. "It's your turn first," she whispered to me and then left to join the others who sat in the circle around me.

Our scrying bowl, a vessel of water in which to see visions, seemed not like an old cauldron now, but like a magical wishing well. I felt, too, that I was in a different place, and I could barely hear the chants and songs of the others as I concentrated on my scrying. I then felt the urge to place my hand in the water and not surprisingly now, I could not feel the base of the cauldron anymore and the water appeared to be very deep. I felt that I had entered into another realm and I knew that its depths would take me, like a well, to a deeper part of myself. I pulled my hand out of the sparkling-mooned water and watched a dancing lady, dressed in white with tresses of golden braided hair. She beckoned to me from the water and I watched the spirit of me dance with her in the moonlit night. I watched her swing me around; dancing, dancing as if the night had no other purpose. The moon lady danced with me until I was dizzy with whirling and just when I thought I may fall with disorientation, I heard a lyre playing and people laughing. The moon lady swung me around one more time and I saw my wraith self to be dancing in a medieval hall, bedecked with boughs of green and posies of summer flowers. I knew that this was the dance of Beltaine, the welcoming of the May Queen.

I saw the image of my astral self immediately, standing at the far side of the candle lit hall. I looked as if I was waiting for someone, something to happen maybe. My eyes were constantly searching among the hall of impassioned dancers. Everywhere I could hear the swish of ladies' long dresses, laughter and the music of the lyre. The moon lady was now nowhere to be seen.

I studied my wraith self in the deep water; I wore a scarlet velvet dress. As soon as I saw this I knew what I was looking for in the room full of dancers. I was seeking the other in the hall, who wore the same scarlet robe. As I realised this a young man, handsome in stature, held out his hand to me. This I took without even looking at his face. All I noticed was his red velvet robe. He led me out of the heady atmosphere of the hall into a garden covered completely in moss, be-speckled with daisies. It was only when I reached the mossy garden and my partner turned to face me, that I saw that it was Laurie. Now we were secretly standing, hands enfolded with one another and he kissed the wraith of me softly on the lips.

At this I could look no more into the scrying water and I swished my hands violently to banish the images that had been shown to me. I quickly became aware of the others sitting grouped around me, they had ceased their spiralling. The magical well, now looked like the old cauldron once more and I remembered the children's TV programme where Bagpuss would go back to being a saggy old cloth cat after the magic had gone. The magic had disappeared and I was back in the woods with my friends. Laurie was the first to open his eyes, as he heard me swirling the water anxiously. I had stopped momentarily, staring into his glance and he smiled at me, with an uncanny, knowing smile.

He must know, he really must know, I had thought to myself frantically as I picked up the cauldron of sloshing water and passed it to Katri. Laurie must have seen the distress in my face. *What did he know, what was he saying to me with that meaningful smile?* I handed Katri the vessel and she looked around the circle to see who would like to scry next. "Do you want to share anything of what you saw?" she asked me.

"It was Beltaine night. I think that Beltaine this year has left a lasting impression...that is all." I censored my response and resumed my place in the circle. Ned chose to scry into the water and he seemed to become quickly immersed in the experience, as I had done. There was a deep silence inside my head and there were thoughts behind my face that could never be put into real words. A shameful thought collection paraded in my mind for the remainder of the night, as if I was wearing an uncomfortable cloak of tormenting truths.

* * *

That night, back in my own bed I had managed, it seemed to pull the whole creeping-out-while-my-husband-is-asleep business off surprisingly well. Lying next to Michael, my strength of feeling for Laurie scared me. In one way I was asking him to enchant me, and I longed for it. The words; *enchant me; enchant me,* drifted through my mind, over and over, as if they had a life of their own. I constantly imagined that I could feel his touch upon my body, and that we were faeriewitchly making love. These thoughts were beginning to run away with me and my bag of heavy thoughts grew even heavier upon my shoulders, as I watched my husband breathing sleep-fully, next to my own face. I had to close the door on my thoughts, so that they could not be heard. I did not want to face a night of imaginings, with no sleep to be had.

I moved closer to Michael, feeling the smooth, clean sheets beneath me. I kissed his forehead and he uttered a deep sigh in his sleep, and I loved him; oh how I loved him in that moment. However, he seemed to keep me in a box of conventionality, from which I was trying incessantly to break free.

Can you make love in a box?

The words in my mind jumbled and jostled for space to think about Laurie. The words had a way of their own, possessing me by keeping my attention constant upon them.

Can words make love?

Sleep beckoned, sleep flirted with me and eventually I fell into a helter skelter slumber, to escape my own imaginings.

* * *

The next day I was late for work, for I was feeling physically sick with the force of my own emotions. What emotions I am not sure, not

22

even whence they came. I had forgotten what inner peace and tranquillity felt like, for feelings were swirling within me like snakes.

I do not like snakes. They weigh so heavily on my mind, and twist so forcefully around my body, that they do not know how to get out.

I do not know how they got in.

I always say that what you focus on will come true, and that was what I was afraid of. For Laurie had filled my mind and body with thought, it was only a matter of time before thoughts would become a reality. I dreaded and wished for it at the same time, the dread was there because I could not contain the guilt.

The telephone rang and I got up from the sofa to the telephone, which was on a small table in the hallway. "Hello."

"It's me, Laurie." I sat on the floor and rested my head on the wall, closing my eyes at the inescapable destiny of it all. "Are you there?"

"Yes, I'm here." He proceeded to launch into a speech about a book he was reading, completely missing out the pleasantries of small talk, which would usually begin our telephone conversations.

"You must, must read it Jessa. It's about two people who are in love, in this strange place in the future, but they never tell one another that they are in love. They have an affair, but not in reality, it's in another dimension or something. You know that people in the future, when in fiction are always telepathic aren't they? Well this was one step further and they were actually there in this unreal place, even though they weren't, if you see what I mean?"

"I know what you mean, carry on." At that moment it occurred to me that he was drunk or stoned, probably the latter, because he was talking extremely quickly and with great confidence. This only happened to Laurie, when he was either drunk or stoned; the rest of the time, when under the influence of his own personality, he was usually reticent and sometimes even withdrawn.

"They meet in this other place and have a love affair and there is a line in the book: I can't remember it word for word, but he says to her, why bother risking everything in reality, when you can experience one another in unreality just the same." He seemed to stop talking abruptly and there was a short uneasy, thinking, breathing silence. My mind was going overtime, for now I knew that the archaeologist had received my thought parcel, intact and in full Technicolor. "I thought you would be at work today?" he asked, for something to fill the pause.

"Why did you phone me, if you expected me to be out?"

"I just rang on the off chance that you may be there, but I did think that I would get your answer machine, but..." he paused. "I wasn't going to leave a message, just in case the wrong person heard it." His voice now sounded more serious and the excitement had faded from it. He didn't ask me why I was not at work and I did not volunteer the information either. There was another pause, not so drawn out this time, and as if remembering his stoned persona, he propelled the conversation into his ebullient mood once more. He talked quickly, hardly daring to take breaths, about another book he was reading; it was about men and the reawakening of the Goddess within the male psyche. I felt hypnotised by his voice and refreshed to hear a man talking so passionately and sensitively on such a prohibited subject among men. While listening to him I imagined him; how he was sitting, what clothes he was wearing. I was captivated by him in those moments, and the knowing that he had received my thought parcel, made me smile inside.

Our unspoken, un-touching love affair had now been acknowledged, when I had scryed at the previous night's ritual had his wraith body been with me? I was so sure of the fact that we had met and could meet in another time-place, that the thought of it sent a deep tingle throughout my entire body. It seemed almost more exciting than embarking on a love affair in the flesh. Until now, I had convinced myself that only my body thought of him, only my body wanted and esteemed him.

Lying to myself is a particular gift of mine, for I had been contemplating a love affair in actuality, one that would involve guilt and would hurt Michael. However, who can be found guilty of thoughts, unless they are spoken? Thoughts can stay inside and always be kept within; they can never be found out, if you want them to stay a secret. For who has yet invented a machine that can record or take pictures of a person's thoughts? As I had found out, thoughts could be sent and received by people in harmony with one another. Now I wanted to find out if thoughts could be experienced by two people at the same time and with the same intensity. This was to be an experiment in thinking and feeling, of which I might never know the other participants findings.

As soon as our telephone conversation had ended, I ran into the kitchen and took my blue glass bowl I used for scrying, filled it with water and then placed it in the centre of the kitchen floor. I then prepared and cast a circle around myself, swishing the water around with my hands until I felt dizzy and disorientated with the eagerness of my intent.

"For goodness sake, tell me if I am right, tell me if I am right please," I whispered into the bowl of water, as I immersed my hands into the cool liquid. The reaction was instant, for my perception of reality altered to such a degree, that I nearly fell from the giddiness of the feeling. The water my hands were in was not now clear, tap water, but water that was alive, swimming with pond creatures, breathing with pond weed and lilies in a murky green colour. I gasped at the sudden change in the water and immediately wanted to take my hands from it, as I could feel fish and tadpoles swimming in-between my fingers. However, to find my truth, I knew that they had to stay put. The bottom of the glass bowl felt like silty mud and my knees no longer knelt on my hard kitchen floor, but felt to be kneeling on damp mossy ground.

I opened my eyes, feeling giddy from the change of environment, the altered dimension. I was now experiencing a time within our own realm, a glimpse of a time perhaps. I was peering through a window from our time, to see and experience another space in our mysterious world. When I opened my eyes, I was surprised to see something in the murky water, for the colour was so dense. It was as if the sunshine was glinting upon a summer's pond and this was allowing me to see. I watched a faerie man, dressed in leather wraps with long hair, summon me with his seeking eyes. As before, I saw the spirit of me, known to us in the Ring as the *fetch,* dance on the mossy bank. My faerie man was taller than I and he smelled of the earth, of the woodlands and he sparked the magic within me as we danced. I was in awe of his presence and could only look into his ruddy coloured, soft featured face, as we danced and danced. I do not recall any music, although it seemed as if there was music as we reeled and whirled. He spoke no words, but I could feel his thoughts penetrate my mind.

I saw the spirit of me wearing the same deep scarlet velvet dress. As soon as I noticed the scarlet robe, my faerie man was nowhere to be seen and I could hear the music of a lyre and laughter in the distance. Instead of holding the hands of the faerie man, my hands were clasped with those that I recognised. I was still dancing, barefooted now on the mossy ground, be-speckled with tiny flowers. At first, I only noticed my dancing partner's clothes; he wore the same vermillion velvet tunic as me. Our dancing slowed softly to a stand still, where our arms enfolded around one another. I saw his face it was, of course Laurie's, as I had hoped and expected. He kissed the spirit of me deeply, and as I watched these watery impressions I could not swish the water to erase the images that I was witnessing. I watched, mesmerised at our togetherness, our velveteened bodies, both wanting the other.

Eventually the spell was broken and I knew that the real world beckoned. Before leaving for work an hour late, I telephoned feigning a migraine that had now eased off. The sun shone weakly through the clouds as I caught the bus from Chesham Bois to the neighbouring market town of Chesham. I always got off a couple of stops early, late or not, so that I could walk the short distance to work through the Old Town district.

Rapunzel, Rapunzel, let your hair down! I felt to be entrapped in a tower, woven from a cobweb of my own emotions. I was the one who had placed myself there and I was the one who had swallowed the key. The only way to escape was to break the glass, but when I had done so, I hadn't wanted to climb out, for it had looked such a long way down. I saw the moon's dew from my spying place. Sparkling on the broken glass, it caught the elusive light and beckoned to me. The glass had been shattered and I was now exposed, nude. I could see out, but nobody could see in. How peculiar a place this was, that even through splintered glass, nobody seemed to notice what went on, within my watchtower. A tower is a safe place to be, even if it is dark, for nothing can touch you, but yourself. I have found that the self keeps within it a myriad of doors, tunnels and pits to be explored, if you have the courage to face them. Those of us, who are tunnelling on a journey within, are not usually doing it by choice, but at knife point, or for fear of falling into the snake pit.

The library where I worked was situated very near the old part of the town. As I walked through the special atmosphere that only Church Street can evoke, my pace slowed to an idle dawdle, as I peered into the old houses. This was my usual occupation when walking to work; the first reason being, that this was the final part of the journey and anything to delay the time when I arrived at work was to be welcomed. The second reason was, that being in Chesham Old Town, transported me to another time and any time other than now interested me. Even though all the houses directly faced the pavement, with no gardens or driveways to block the view from passers-by, hardly any of them had net curtains. This meant a splendid view was had, as I walked slowly to work each day, after the short bus ride. I would see lolloping fat cats on plush sofas and chaise longues and pianos with music open at a page, as if someone had just finished practising. Old ladies with lace covered tea trays and china tea sets, would sit by their radios and I fancied, listen to radio plays.

All these houses had three storeys and a cellar to them, and their floors sloped and their ceilings were low and beamed. They were cosy houses with even more ordinary occupants, and the little timeless world that they created, on the last five minutes before I reached the library sometimes sustained me all day. My imagination would ponder on everything that I had seen and delighted in, and I would think on what it would have been like to live in such a house at the time it had been built.

I hurried on to the library and found that this mornings' work meant that I could gratefully shut myself away in the reference library's office to order some books for the poetry section. My mind meandered as I worked methodically, for I knew that Michael would not come home tonight at all. He was staying in a hotel for a couple of nights, because of a conference he was attending in Edinburgh. His job, working for a publishing company, often took him away from home and I did miss him. He left the house making it feel unfulfilled and hollow. Books were the only thing that we had in common with one another, except that his interest in them was far more commercial than my own. Business stimulated and invigorated Michael; it just so happened that his business was in books, but it could have been in anything, as long as it involved a mobile phone, a personal organiser and copious lunches out with clients.

Michael Fawn was twelve years older than myself, and I had met him when I was only twenty and I was still at university. What I had seen in him was a passport to a different kind of life. He seemed to take the dullness and the foreseeable out of my life and replace it with a compelling spirit with everything that he did. What I had not realised, was that Michael would not allow me to become absorbed in his life. I watched him carry on his vigorous career, as if I was a spectator, watching breathlessly and admiringly at every move; for I adored the being of Michael, but we lived for the most part, self-contained lives, meeting only in bed and sometimes at weekends. Emptiness was a feeling that I was used to; it clothed my body and every part of our home. We did communicate when he was away, but Michael did not send me love letters, be-ribboned and covered with kisses. He sent me emails that would greet me in his office at home. Sending emails is not the natural inclination for a hoarder of love letters, such as me, for electronic messages, once read are simply wiped into the ether and vanish, unless you print them out.

I had once asked him, while sitting on the beach together on a holiday to Italy, what he had first seen in me. He did not seem to have to think about his answer, but said immediately, "Your vulnerability."

"What if I stop being vulnerable, perhaps I just haven't grown up enough, what then?" I had asked, running the white-hot sand through my fingers.

"Because then, you'll still be a mystery to me Jessa. I don't know anything more about you, than the first day we met," he had watched me as he said this, his boyish face suddenly becoming serious.

"Of course you know me, don't be ridiculous, you see everything that I am."

"I only see what you want me to see, and I doubt that that will change."

"It's an unconscious thing." I answered impetuously, knowing that he had pressed a button I thought was invisible to the human eye.

"I know that," he said "I like everything that you have chosen to show me and what I first saw in you, still attracts me."

I read the same sentence for what must have been the fifth time, on the poetry list of new titles, as I remembered our Italian holiday, when we had been new to one another. Michael loved and revered me, but he could not help me to climb out of my watch tower. He used to peer in the narrow windows, but now he did not even look, or even remember that there was a tower, he was too involved within his career. He saw that I was amusing myself without him and he felt happy with that, for he admired an enquiring spirit, even if he did not understand what I was seeking. He could not have tolerated a clingy wife and he needed to know that I was independent enough to exist happily without him when he was not around - which was often. However, he could not understand that my independence would carry on when he was at home too.

Until Laurie …

The name Laurie seemed to be electrically charged, as I tumbled it over in my mind, again and again, the power in the name transfixing my thoughts.

"Jessamyn," I heard a familiar voice say, and I looked up a little startled. "You're always somewhere else, wherever you are." It was Ned, poking his head around the office door.

"And why ever not?" I answered.

"Of course, why be somewhere dull, when you can be somewhere unreal and far more exciting?" he asked, shutting the door behind him. He wore tatty and faded blue jeans and an even more lived in looking T-shirt. He had some of his hair braided in rainbow strands and he looked as if he hadn't shaved for a few days. He perched himself on the edge of my desk, moving a few papers to accommodate himself and folding his arms he said; "It's all arranged."

"What is?" I asked putting my pen down.

"Velvet's downstairs looking at books in the lending library and she said if you say its okay, I can sit in on your apprentice session this evening." He picked up my poetry list and started to read it.

"Let's paraphrase; you've talked her into it and made her wait downstairs while you butter me up?"

"The answer's yes then?" He grinned, handing me back my poetry list.

"I don't see how it can hurt, as long as Velvet doesn't mind."

"Stop worrying. Now what time do you finish here?"

"Five-thirty."

"That was fifteen minutes ago, so let's get out of here." He took the pen out of my hand and placed it on the desk. "I can help you with the training, after you've fed me of course." He smirked at my reaction. "Don't worry, I'll cook." He playfully took my hand, gently pulling me out of the office.

"It's a good job I know you so well Ned Middleton. Luckily I've known you long enough to know that you're not in the least bit joking," I said following him down the stairs.

"Ah, but I will give you a lift home Milady," he said touching an imaginary cap and grinning.

"Thank you Middleton, how very kind." I grinned.

Once at home Ned busied himself by searching through all my kitchen cupboards out of sheer nosiness and also for something to cook for dinner. I could hear him whistling a tune as he clanged and crashed his way through my kitchen. His methods were erratic, but his culinary efforts were quite delicious. That night Ned brought to my house an energy which I only found in other people who shared my magical ways. I had felt drained today as work at the library had taken the very essence of me.

Velvet and I had both perched ourselves cross-legged on my deep and squashy sofa. She had on her lap a pen and notepad, poised to take down notes and I began to look at my file of all Kel and Katri's notes of what I was meant to cover in her apprenticeship as a Faerie Priestess. "I suppose we'd better get down to some work. Now it seems that the first thing we need to tackle is the creation of your *Book of Elfin*, which is your personal magical diary...oh, bollocks I really can't stick this. Velvet, I've got something to show you, if you're up for it that is?" I threw my file and pens down onto the sofa and got up. Velvet's eyes widened and then she smiled and got up too.

"Definitely up for it."

"Ned we're going out for half an hour, we'll be back for dinner," I explained poking my head around the kitchen door.

"Where are you going?" he asked, momentarily pausing as he chopped an onion.

"I'll tell you when we get back, it's just apprentice stuff."

"Kelsey never takes me out on apprentice nights."

"Kelsey goes by the book and that's just not my way."

"Well just make sure you are back by seven or it will be burnt."

"Okay, don't get your pinny in a twist, we'll be back." I grabbed Velvet's hand as we went out the back door, heading on the path which led to the woods.

"Jessa, do you think...I hope you don't mind me asking?"

"Ask."

"Do you think Ned is gay?"

I laughed. "Oh no, he's definitely not gay, but he will make someone a very good wife someday. I think his mother is a brilliant cook and it rubbed off on him."

"He really took me under his wing at Uni. I think I must have just looked lost in the corridor one day in Fresher's week and we've been friends ever since."

"Ned has wonderful and unusual qualities." I quickened my pace as we turned a corner on the footpath and the woods had just come into view. "We're nearly there."

Velvet had to run a little to keep up with me. For some reason, which I could not put my finger on, I could feel an excitement rising within me and I knew, beyond all doubt that *they* would be waiting for us.

The suburban pathway, lined with terraced Georgian houses gave way to a dirt track which led to the woods. I could feel the dampness and rich earthiness of the air change as we took the public footpath. "Am I allowed to ask where we are going?"

"It's difficult to explain. It's somewhere in the woods, but I won't know we're there until I get there. Sorry that just didn't make sense, you'll see soon." We walked silently along the footpath and in the early evening the gnats and midges were gathering around our heads. It was a pleasant May evening and the sun was still warm upon us. There was no one else about and all we could hear were the sounds of the woods; of the leaves gently rustling and birds. As we entered the woods, I knew this was the place where my gods dwelt and I held reverence for the trees around me.

"I want to show you where the Faerie Ring works and I think it's just up here past this tree stump." We stopped in our tracks as if we had to have permission to enter. "We all call this *The Magic Place*, it's just the name that stuck. This is where we gather to work all of our outdoor rites when the weather is good enough." The Magic Place was a circle of mature trees of many varieties, which circled a small dip or dell as we called it and it was perfect in every way, as if it had been purposefully created. It was sheltered from the breeze, so that we could light our candles; and being in a dell, we were also hidden from view from passers-by. It was surrounded by a thick undergrowth of nettles, brambles and ferns and was well off the public footpath. This meant that we seemed to be the only ones who entered it and we often had to beat a path to the dell with our faerie besoms to gain entrance in the summer months.

Velvet and I stood at the edge of The Magic Place just looking at the circle of trees, which held a peculiar kind of stillness all of its own. "If I tell you this Velvet, can you promise me not to tell any one else? All of our apprentice sessions are confidential by the way and go no further than the Faerie Ring. No one outside the Ring must know the whereabouts of The Magic Place, but there's something else too."

"I can promise," she whispered intently looking into my eyes.

"It is only sometimes that we can find this dell. Often we come here to leave some flowers or an offering of honey to the Faerie Queen and we simply cannot find the dell. We take the same pathway each time and quite often it's just not here."

"So what's in its place?"

"Random trees and nettles, but no dell or circle of trees like this. It's as if this dell is really a place between the worlds and sometimes we are allowed to stumble upon it and others we are not. There have been a couple of occasions when the entire Ring has lost it and we have had to go and work somewhere else in the woods. Other times some of us have found it and others haven't and someone has to come looking for the missing members to show them where it is. It happened to me in the ritual only last night and Kel came to find me."

"Spooky. So I'm honoured then?"

"Yes, but so am I. It's as if it will only show itself to you when it's absolutely necessary."

"There must be a good reason?"

At that moment the peculiar silence that held itself suspended in The Magic Place grew a little more peculiar. It was as if the air had become thicker and the only thing that existed was the dell within the circle of trees. The rest of the woodland seemed to have diminished in our perceptions and all that held our attention was The Magic Place magnified a thousand times in depth and curiosity. Velvet and I exchanged glances for a fleeting moment, when the sound of beautiful music brought our attentions back to the dell. What met our gaze was the woodland copse blinking with bright eyes, brimming with aliveness - a place forbidden. The eyes looked like dozens of cat's eyes peering through the gaps in the leaves at us.

The music could not be disunited from the breeze and at some moments I could not make a distinction between the sound of the wind and the hypnotic music.

Velvet and I crept forward a little closer to the copse and knelt right at the edge of the clearing. To my astonishment, two of the pairs of cat-like eyes came out from the security of the leaves. They were surrounded by forms of silvery, misty light. These light forms began to dance in the dell, prancing high and bright, as if they were a part of the breeze. It was then that I felt Velvet's hand squeeze mine, as if she needed reassurance. I could not take my gaze away from this curious and entrancing sight.

It was then that the prancing beings of light took on form and slowly their elfin bodies looked as if they were solid. It was only their hands and feet which gave them away, as they were tapered and disappeared at the ends into the very breeze, as a silvery sparkling mist. The two elfin beings danced before us as lovers and we were both utterly transfixed, as if we were under a spell ourselves. They looked like an elfin king and queen with their shimmering garments and crowns that glimmered in the golden evening rays of sunlight.

Their dance began to move more intensely and suddenly they were not only dancing, but making sensual love, performing a Faerie Great Rite of intensity and making love, not only to one another, but to themselves, the rays of sunlight and the woodland around them. They were embracing everything as well as one another, sending showers of sparkling light to illuminate the dell. Surrounding their bright bodies was the music too, as if it were a swirling object and I could almost see the music be-ribboning the dancers. I had never seen such an honouring and revelry of two beings, who seemed to be totally in tune with the movements and feelings of one another and also the seen and unseen dimensions of their surroundings. I could not help but be moved and I knew that they were dancing this dance for everyone; for all of nature and for humanity. For without faeries the days would not be bright and the moon would glide alone in an empty, starless sky. Their dancing is to aliveness as nuns are to prayer and they inject the sparkle into the Earth and into our beings.

I was enjoying the fey spectacle of passion and beauty and had quite forgotten that within the unexpected experience I had to remember a surprise when I was least expecting it – and that moment was upon me.

One moment I was watching the elfin queen, the next I *was* her. The shape-shifting encounter can have only lasted a split second, but in that fragment of a second was a cavern of time. I found myself holding both hands facing the elfin king, the gentlest and most sensual being. He smiled his elfin smile and winked at me in the sexiest gesture I will ever receive, conveying his desire for me and I felt the most revered woman in the universe. He did not have to physically touch me to make love to me, as I felt his beautiful fingers glide over my waiting skin, although he was still holding my hands. I felt arousal like I had never experienced it before, as if I was going to burst with desire and then I felt filled with the universe; the stars, the breeze, as the god energy had entered me.

Velvet squeezed my hand and I realized that I was back. "They went," she whispered.

"Yes," was all I could manage to whisper back, looking at The Magic Place which was now just a dell in the woods.

"I think they reached a climax, that's what it looked like and then the whole scene vanished, as if it had never appeared." Velvet let go of my hand and stared at the copse for a few moments, as if that would summon them back from their realms. There was a long silence between us, and neither of us moved because we knew that would break the spell. A robin redbreast broke it for us, as it pecked at the moss by our feet.

"I'm never going to be the same again," whispered Velvet.

"You've entered the weird, weird of weirdness that goes with being in the Faerie Ring. You can escape now, relatively unscathed or carry on down the moss-lined pathway."

"I'm up for weirdness."

"I thought you might be. You have kind of begun in at the deep end I would say, but now at least you have something to write about for your first entry in your new Book of Elfin." We both giggled and I secretly felt weirder than I had ever felt in my life and if there is such as thing as psychic shock, I think I was in it.

"Do you think dinner will be burnt?"

"Ned!" I gasped standing up suddenly. "We must have been much longer than half an hour, we'll have to run." We ran back along the footpath giggling so much that we kept stumbling and almost falling over. We burst through the door and gorgeous cooking smells greeted our senses. "Sorry Ned!" I yelled and he appeared at the kitchen door.

"For what, have you forgotten something?"

He asked with a bemused expression. "We forgot the time. We just got caught up in something you see. I hope dinner isn't too burnt?"

"I hope not either; it's only just gone in the oven. I mean, you've only been twenty minutes, give me a chance." Velvet and I exchanged furtive glances.

"What's up?" he asked.

"It could be a side-effect."

"Of what?" he asked with the distinct expression of someone who has missed out on something yet again.

"You could say we bumped into a happening and that stretchy-time-thing that sometimes happens in the Ring … well … happened."

"That explains it all then," he uttered sarcastically. "I knew I should have gone with you."

Chapter Three

The Dreaming

'How life and love are all a dream…'

Robert Burns, The Lament

A week later Velvet stood smiling expectantly on my doorstep in the dusky evening light. "You are Ned-less," I observed as she made her way into my lounge.

"He said he was busy."

"Well I hope he's along later, because he's supposed be giving me a lift to Coombe Hill."

"What are you doing there?"

"The Faerie Ring are camping for the night there and holding a ritual beforehand. It just means that we don't have to worry about what time we finish and anybody that wants to drink at the feast afterwards can just crash out. It works out quite nicely usually; we hold them from time to time."

"I can't wait until I can come along to the rituals," she said as she plonked herself down on my sofa which almost seemed to envelop her slim frame. "What are we doing today then?"

"We're going to journey to Elphame by way of a meditation. Although, this time it won't be by accident, we're going there quite on purpose. You just need to listen to my voice and I'll guide you through the journey."

"Do you do it, or are you just the escort, so to speak?"

"I will journey with you because it's difficult not to visualize the meditation while I'm speaking it, but I won't go as deep as you. I'll keep a certain part of myself back." I sat down on the other end of the sofa.

"I think Ned would have enjoyed this, it's a shame he's going to miss it, although I'm sure he's done it all before in his own training."

"Maybe, maybe not, everyone teaches differently and we all add our own touches for every apprentice. Now close your eyes take a few deep breaths and relax. Leave your day behind and concentrate on finding the still place within you." Velvet relaxed with ease as I began to take her through the meditation to Faerie Land.

As I guided her through the meditation my thoughts began to wander and my mind drifted to the events of *the Remembering*. With the advent of this spiritual experience it was as if I had shifted my life suddenly into some sort of clairvoyant acceleration. It had all definitely begun with Laurie and I being crowned as the Faerie Ring's King and Queen of Cobwebs.

Re-cap. So far all in the space of about three weeks I had fallen in love with another man, by what had felt like some kind of divine intervention. He had then appeared to me in place of my husband while making love, ooh and I mustn't forget to mention *the Remembering* and the elfin king and queen lovers I had seen with Velvet in The Magic Place. To add to the weirdness, it was now looking pretty likely that I was involved with Laurie in a Maud Gonne and W.B.Yeats feel-a-like astral love affair. Ever since that enchanted Beltaine night my life had taken on a heightened quality and I was seeing the unseen, whether I comprehended the insights that I was experiencing or not. I felt as if I had now moved into a new phase of being, where the world of faerie was nearer and more visible to me than ever before. I was walking my pathway in life with one foot in this world and the other in the fey realm of secrets. Why this had happened I did not yet know, but I did know that all these experiences were inextricably linked to Laurie.

I wondered if he too, (as well as experiencing the astral connection which we were both having), had moved into a new phase of spiritual encounters? *The Remembering* bugged me from the perspective that although on the surface I knew its meaning for me, I felt that it had a wider significance; that as yet I did not understand. Why had I been shown *the Remembering*- and why at the very beginning of my heightened clairvoyant experiences? Was it the gateway to the meaning of the phase I was going through?

Pondering was something I was getting used to in these last few weeks. I absently wrote *the Remembering* down on the writing pad that rested on my knees. I needed to discover its true hidden meaning and I did not feel as if I could rest until I had.

"Now bring yourself back to the here and now and in your own time you can your eyes," I explained, bringing the visualization to a close. Velvet's eyelids flickered momentarily as if she could not decide whether she wanted to come back or not. Then she grinned and opened her sparkly brown eyes.

"That was just beautiful; I don't think I've ever felt so relaxed. I really did enjoy that."

"I thought you might," I grinned too. "I'll go and put the kettle on; you need something to bring yourself back to earth."

"Jessamyn?" she asked and I halted in the doorway, turning to face her. "This doesn't feel like how I thought it was going to feel."

"How do you mean?"

"I really thought that I was going to prove myself wrong and that all this faerie stuff was going to turn out to be something that I could sort out. I wanted to square it with the faeries and do whatever they were trying to grab my attention for and then most definitely get on with a normal life. I get the impression that the faeries just don't work like that do they? What I mean to say is that since I have been working with you and since meeting everyone in the Faerie Ring, everything in my life that wasn't quite right, now just seems to be slipping into place, as if I've found the missing ingredient that I never knew was missing. It just all feels so right: am I making sense?"

"You are a natural, Velvet, so it makes every sense. So if it feels right, just go with it. I think the place of faerie is where you most definitely belong."

"You think so?"

There was a knock at the front door; I winked at Velvet and then went to answer it. There stood Ned on the doorstep holding up a bottle of red wine and smiling cheekily with his boyish lop-sided grin. "So tell me I've missed everything," he said.

"You've missed everything," I replied laughing, "but we'll cancel that cup of tea and have your wine instead." I took the wine from his hands as he walked into the lounge. "How can I have missed everything again?"

"Call it knack." I answered and he kissed me warmly on both cheeks.

"That must be it, Oh Queen of Cobwebs, that must be it," and he too plonked himself down on my sofa next to Velvet.

"Can I get you both a drink then?"

Ned had mistakenly sat down on my writing pad and as he retrieved it from underneath him, he glanced at what I had written. "What have I been missing then, what's this all about, Jess; *the Remembering*? I certainly haven't covered that with Kel."

"No, no you wouldn't have. It's nothing to do with the apprentice session, just something I've been pondering on over the last few weeks, it was a name I gave to an experience I had recently."

"Sorry, I didn't think it was private when I read it. Are we allowed to know about it?"

"Oh it's okay, it's not a secret, I just didn't know if telling anyone else could shed anymore light on it, that's all."

"Why don't we all ponder on it together with the Ring tonight?"

I nodded in agreement and secretly wished that I had not left that pad around. I hadn't meant it to become a Faerie Ring conference subject, although I knew that Ned was only trying to be helpful.

As I went to the kitchen to open Ned's bottle of wine, I popped my head around Michael's office door to check if there were any emails from him, as I had not heard from him all day. Indeed, there was one waiting for me and it read;

Hi Jessa, ignore yesterday's email, because my plans have changed. The conference has been exceptionally dull, except for one thing, I have met a very interesting literary agent and I have been invited to stay with him for a couple of days in Edinburgh. I hope to be home Tuesday night, a bit later that you expected

He went on to list his flight number, flight times and the address where he was staying. As I read the email, typed accurately in perfect Michael style, I missed his presence in the house and his steadying influence on my life. Although his frequent absence made my freedom available, I wasn't always sure that I wanted it. What I had always wanted was Michael and no other distractions. There was less explaining to do while he was away, fewer feelings of guilt and more magical experiences. However, Michael-less time was time to explore the mind and other people's minds and when he was not there, he was less likely to keep me away from distractions (attractions). I was constantly like Alice-in-Wonderland, falling so very deep and fast, but not forgetting to wonder at things along the way.

It was still light, dusk just beginning to turn towards night, as Ned and I climbed out of his car after the short journey to Coombe Hill, near Wendover in Buckinghamshire, after having first dropped Velvet off at her home. As we shut the car doors Kel stood at the far end of the car park. "Over here," he beckoned and I could see Laurie standing next to him, oblivious to his surroundings, an open paperback in one hand and a cigarette in the other, immersed in his reading. Ned heaved our rucksacks out of the boot of the car and we walked over to join Kel, Katri and Laurie. Kel and Katri leant over and kissed me on both cheeks. "Laurie was sensible; he came prepared for a wait," said Kel glancing at Laurie who looked up momentarily from his book and grinned.

"Anyone got a spare tent?" He asked, snapping his book shut.

"What happened to yours?" asked Ned.

"It's gone to Bognor Regis on a scout camp with my twelve year old nephew. I've borrowed a sleeping bag from Kel, but so far, it looks as though I will be sleeping under the stars."

"You can share with me. I've got a two-man tent and I suppose Jessa and Katri will be sharing. What about you Ned?" asked Kel.

"I'm borrowing Jessamyn's, I didn't chauffeur her here for nothing," he grinned patting his bulging rucksack, in which the tent was packed.

"Shall we go and find a pitch before it starts to get really dark?" suggested Laurie. We all lit our lanterns with the aid of Laurie's lighter and then together, we made our way through a thickly wooded area. Our little gathering was a quietly merry one, as we all set off in the closing darkness, giggling, chatting and joking. We led one another by the hand through bramble bushes and over fallen trees. After about ten minutes walking, we found ourselves in a small clearing, surrounded on all sides by trees. Here our tents would be secretly enfolded within the woodland, with only our flickering lanterns to give us away.

The night prickled electrically with happenings to come, as we set about erecting the three tents, fumbling about in the darkness as the night grew deeper.

Now was when I could thrive, where I could drink in the mood of my thought-filled knot of friends and search the gaps in time. Katri lit some heady incense in a tree stump, covered in fungi and moss. We then all placed our lanterns around the stump, encircling the spiralling smoke in light. We had all gathered around Katri's centre piece, in the mutual silence, every one of us in awe at the night's intoxicating atmosphere.

We were on the threshold of magic and our bodies and thoughts tingled with our collective aliveness in anticipation of what was to come.

Spontaneously, we all clasped hands at the same time, smiling silently at one another, our auras intermingling in our circle of expectancy. Kel drew a deep breath and looked around at us all and as he did so Laurie squeezed my hand and my feelings swirled dangerously inside me. It was as if he was reassuring me, for we were all passengers on a roller coaster ride and the lights were amber, about to go green. I believed that my Archaeologist and I would soon meet in the place where clocks could not tick.

Kel smiled broadly and said quietly, almost under his breath; "let's cast the faerie circle." There the real world ended and my Archaeologist began to dig for my words, and then catch them in a spider's web; the web that catches secrets, catches dreams. The place between two worlds stood tempting us now, its door wide open, waiting and wanting. We knew that we should enter through the deep red door, lest we should miss our chance.

After the Ring had cast the circle, we five seekers trod the spiral; slowly and methodically we cast our energy to enter Faerie Land. We could almost see the spiral pathway that we were treading, such was its tangibility, journeying to the in-between place; our faerie destination. It was as if the trees watched us, listening and whispering in the gentle breeze. We had now all reached the altered state that we had set out to achieve. Our ritual that night was to celebrate the full moon and as I peered up in between the trees there was the pale moon looking down upon us all.

Suddenly a familiar sensation overcame me. I felt as if my legs had become the roots of a tree, my torso felt like bark and my outstretched arms were rigid. I felt myself sink lower and the warm earth, envelope my roots. I felt as if I was in earth up to my waist and I could no longer hear the chanting of the others, but only the hushed murmuring of the trees. I could see swirling coloured lights, twist and dance in and out of the trees and the knowledge of the earth's wisdom seemed to be entrapped within my woody being. The experience was all encompassing, totally exhilarating and yet it was still and silent, quietly potent and all feeling. I did not wish to escape from this experience, despite its scary sensations, for I knew it to be the land's own way of accepting me.

I opened my eyes for a short moment, briefly aware that the others were all in trance too. What I saw, was each one in our Ring standing still, with their eyes closed, clearly experiencing the same as I. Each of our bodies was covered in a green light, which also surrounded our circle and the encircling trees. My mind wandered as I closed my eyes, as I fell into what felt like a deep sleep, but I knew it to be a journey through the open red door. I was entering my place, the gap where reality stops and the thought spider weaves her web. Beyond the door, I could travel through time, mostly in a linear fashion, unlike sleep, exciting drugs or madness. This was different now, I wasn't seeing my astral self in a scrying bowl; I *was* my astral self and I had left my body. My archaeologist stood beyond the red door, and he beckoned to me, as I stood on the threshold of unreality. "Bring your dangerous self with you," he whispered from the other side of the door.

"I take it with me wherever I go," I called back to him.

He held his hand out, but I did not give him my own. I hesitated for a moment, wondering if I should stop all this right now, before it got too messy for me to save myself.

"Take my hand, if not for you, then for me."

"For you? What are you getting out of all this?"

"An experience ... and..."

"And?"

"A part of you, the astral part of you, which is my passport to the Land of Faerie. You are the one who can grant me entry there. You, and only you." He said this as if it was a confession, as if he felt he was using me and he looked as though he wanted to add something in explanation, but couldn't find the words.

"As long as we both know what we're doing I suppose. Is this reality now or merely our imaginations performing our desires before our eyes?"

"This is our reality and no one else's. Nobody else can see it or know it." Again he held out his hand for me to take it again. "We've been waiting for a window from our reality; it won't be here for long. What have you got to lose? Nobody can find us out, because it isn't happening in their reality. How can anyone punish you for something that never took place?" He paused and looked at me directly, so that I could not avoid his gaze. "Take my hand," his hand reached forward to me, palm outstretched, as if it was a bridge to the other world, "Please?"

I slowly and wordlessly, placed my hand in his and as skin touched skin, a delicious lurching shot through my insides. It felt right to be with him, it felt bewitching to be holding his hand. As he led me through the red door, I found myself in a forest; my feet were bare now and so were his. Our clothes had changed, *as if by magic*, I wore a long, heavy brown velvet dress and he a robe in the same fabric. Hand in hand, we walked slowly together along a clear pathway, the springy forest floor under foot. Where we were heading, neither of us knew, but my body tingled with anticipation as I felt him squeeze my hand. We spoke no words, but our feelings and auras intermingled and the forest we were in, seemed to be conscious and sensitive to us. It was as if we were within a magical forest, with qualities akin to a children's fairy tale. The air felt so dense with thoughts and happenings to come, that I could almost have rubbed the air - like a silken scarf, between my fingers.

Time didn't seem to exist here, things happened in a linear way, but everything seemed to be existing in its own presence, being unaware of artificial measurements like time and dates. Laurie and I came to a shallow flowing stream, where the water looked magical, as it glistened and winked with the last rays of sunlight.

It was still daylight here; the forest was in another place, another existence. We both lay down on the mossy banks of the stream, side by side and still with our hands clasped together. "Wow, can you feel them here?" asked Laurie looking around at the trees.

"In a circle all around us."

As I answered him I could sense -encircling us- a group of nature spirits. At first they appeared as a misty, sparkling light. As we watched the mist swirl, the lights began to take shape as faerie beings, indistinct in their outlines, seemed to smudge and merge into one another and into the trees themselves. Their eyes slanted with the knowledge of faerie and I felt we were expected. Laurie and I simply watched taking in our most entrancing welcoming party, transfixed by their proximity.

After a while they seemed to fade away, I cannot explain it in any other way. It was as if they had only been a dream or imagination, maybe they were. For a moment the forest seemed still, as if waiting for something to happen. Laurie and I looked up at the cloudless sky, waiting for what, we could not say. To be shown the way, perhaps. Then something caught my eye and I turned to see a faerie girl getting out of the water on the other side of the stream. "I think she's a nix," whispered Laurie in my ear. "I've read about those, you know they're water spirits."

"Are they of the fey then?"

"They are water faeries. They are known to inhabit either rivers of the Land of Faerie or wishing wells." My heart jolted as he mentioned a well and my mind instantly leapt back to the night of the Faerie Ring ritual in the woods when I first scryed and saw Laurie and I together. I had felt that the cauldron of water had been a wishing well.

"Do you know anymore about them?" I had asked, intrigued.

"Only that they are mischievous, and that the female nixie lure mortal men to be their lovers."

She wore sparkling raindrops in her long dark hair and she was clothed in a weed-green dress, which touched her bare toes. She ran her fingers through her hair and a scattering of sparkling stars fell into her hands. She smiled at me and then threw the stars into the stream. Laurie impulsively jumped to his feet and slid down the mossy bank, plunging his bare feet into the shallow stream. He caught the stars as they floated towards him, scooping them up in his hands. The water trickled through his fingers, as he held the stars, their brilliant light reflecting on his face. Then he climbed out of the stream and knelt down beside me, he began to comb my hair with his fingers and then he plaited the night stars into my hair. The romantic gesture took my breath away.

"Thank you." I said turning to face him, hardly able to take it all in. He touched my face with his fingertips and kissed me on the lips, a soft shy kiss, a beguiling kiss that I fell into without hesitation.

"She's beckoning us," he said, turning to look at the enchanting nixie girl on the opposite side of the stream. The Nix was beginning to slip her long, weedy dress off, letting it drop onto the forest floor. Her body was willowy and it seemed to be covered in, what I fancied was stardust - a luminescence emanating from her body. She beckoned us to take our clothes off as well, and as we did so, our own bodies were covered in the stardust and our skin was alive. We kissed, our bodies quivering with the life force that shone from us. When at last our kiss parted, we turned to see that the Nix had vanished, and only her green dress lay by the bank of the stream.

"Let's run!" exclaimed Laurie, "I've got so much energy, I've got to run." Without waiting for an answer, he took my hand and, laughing we ran, the breeze rushing over our nude, sparkling bodies, the warm grass under our bare feet. As we ran lights crept out of the earth in colours of electric purple, neon red and shimmering white. The colours spiralled around our bodies, as if it were a vine twisting itself in snakes of light. Spiralling, spiralling the colours danced and we ran, ferns whipping our legs as we passed them, we were exhilarated and at one with the earth and with ourselves.

We both stopped and I turned for a moment looking over my shoulder, I saw the Nix's green dress lying by the water's edge in the distance. I wanted to put the dress on; I felt that if I had slipped into it, I would slip into being one with her.

Then maybe I could stay, maybe I would never have to go back and live out my life's drudgery and lies. I turned to face the hidden pathway within the trees, where Laurie had walked. It seemed to beckon me, as it would beckon me back to real life. Glimpsing this place was permissible, but staying here would be to drop out. I knew the rules. Only the privileged experienced life here, and if I took advantage of that privilege, it probably wouldn't turn out to be fantastic after all. Things had a habit of turning out that way with universal laws.

I followed Laurie's footprints and turned the corner to a circle of trees. I stepped within the circle and imagined the Faerie Ring gathering in Coombe Hill woods. I closed my eyes and wished myself back there among friends. Suddenly the temperature changed to a summer night's chill and I heard Katri's voice whispering; "We are all back aren't we?"

"Except Jessa," replied Laurie's voice from beside me. I felt Katri's warm hand touch my own; and I opened my eyes with a start.

"Sorry, did I make you jump? Did I bring you back too soon?" asked Katri, taking her hand away.

"I was here, but not quite, if you see what I mean." I blinked at the bright candle flames before me and Katri nodded and retook her place in the circle.

I stepped willingly into what I always felt was the most beautiful part of our rituals; The Elfin Great Rite. Kel had written this version for a special occasion in the Ring and we had decided to use it in our rituals ever since, for the words were so enchanting.

In the stillness of the night Katri laid herself down, face upwards; facing away from the tree stump altar in the star position. I then placed a white muslin veil over her body and, as I did so she smiled and my long dark hair brushed her body.

Kel knelt dutifully before his Priestess of Elphame, level with her knees. For a moment they just looked into one another's eyes, contemplating the enormity of the act they were about to perform. Katri was the spiritual embodiment of the Faerie Queen, her body the altar and he was the Faerie King performing the sacred marriage in reverence, the key to all life and creativity. Kel slowly raised his arms saying; "As the moon rises over the altar of her body, weave the words with me, the words that will entwine, to the place between the worlds, betwixt the kiss of night and day. We invoke the Enchantress, the Faerie Queen in a stardust body."

He breathed in deeply and Katri replied to him; "We invoke the spellbinder, the Faerie King within an earthly body."

He then lowered his arms and fixed his full gaze on Katri. "The Enchantress we do adore, in the moon wearing her chaplet of stars. Bringing her pleasure wrapped in darkness, to take a potion from me." At his words he removed her veil, in the manner of someone revealing a priceless painting from beneath its cover. He handed the veil to Laurie and I, and in turn I handed him his willow wand. Kel took Katri's hand, and knelt to face him. I handed Katri the chalice, which glinted in the flickering candlelight. Now Katri and Kel were kneeling opposite one another, Kel continued "Without you the moon would not enchant me."

"Without you the sun would not invoke my passion."

"Moon and sun, at the kiss of two worlds." At these words they both closed their eyes and kissed one another on the lips, but it was not Kel and Katri that kissed, it was the Faerie King and Queen. The kiss was a spiritual experience that they fell into, as those succumbing to a prayer that has been answered. This kiss was one that they had performed many times before.

Katri then held up the chalice and Kel lowered the wand, slowly and deliberately into the swirling red wine. "Here the wand and chalice fuse, moon and sun eclipse, Enchantress and Spellbinder meld." He then kissed Katri and they both sipped the wine. The rest of us in the Ring stood on, in awe of the energy that was evoked. Then rising to their feet, the chalice was passed around the Faerie Ring and we all took sips until it was empty. Kel and Katri then consecrated the cakes, which Ned had made in little crescent moons and these were passed around the Ring too. We also left a few on the tree stump altar, as an offering to the faeries and the guardians of the woods.

We all watched silently as Kel banished our faerie circle, as the sun began to rise on our little gathering. We had been in our ritual for the whole night. Strange things happened with time when in a ritual, we could never quite tell what would happen, and tonight had been no exception. In the pale dawn light we all crept into our tents, weary from laughter and exuberance. I think Katri would have liked to talk a little, as we bedded down under the canvas. I was laden with thoughts behind my face and tired from trying to be one thing to myself and another to others.

* * *

When I awoke, the sun was beating down on the canvas and I felt overly hot in my sleeping bag. Katri was not in the tent and I could hear familiar laughter and voices outside. Last night I had dreamt of nothing at all and now I felt refreshed. It was such a relief, not to have thought or experienced anything consciously for a while.

I could hear Laurie's voice amongst the others, and I felt peculiar inside every time he spoke. I pulled the sleeping bag from me and clambered over Katri's sprawled belongings to the zipped up door of the tent. I slowly pulled the zip down a fraction, giving me just enough space so that I could see out, without being seen myself. There they all sat, Kel, Ned, Katri and Laurie, around our makeshift tree stump altar. The men were shirtless and Katri was only wearing her bra with her jeans. She sat with her back to me and I could see her sleek long, black hair hanging perfectly in the middle of her beautiful bare back.

I observed them with interest; it is always fascinating to watch those who believe they are unobserved. Ned and Laurie were smoking and had mugs of coffee in front of them. Kel was listening to an amusing anecdote that Katri was telling to the group. Their eyes shone with liveliness and their skin glistened with the possession of their own sexuality. They were perfectly themselves, as they sat in the sunlight, inspiring the hidden me. I wanted to go and join them, to be a part of their intoxicating oneness, but I knew that to join them, would be to break their spell. So instead, I simply sat and watched from my spying place. I was glad to be there with them, and although I was not engaged with them, I was not lonely.

I sank back from my kneeling position to sit down on my heels. I closed my eyes for a moment, wanting to see Laurie in my mind again. I drifted effortlessly into a mellifluous daydream. Laurie and I were in the woods together, and it didn't seem to be any magical place, as it had seemed before, but simply the Coombe Hill woods, close by to where our tents were. I was slightly in front of him as we walked, and it seemed that he was following me, deeper and deeper into the trees. We eventually turned off the pathway and wended our way around bushes and fallen trees.

I could see a stile a little way in the distance, but as far as I could make out, it was not a stile that was still in use. The wood was covered in lichen and moss, and ivy wound its way around the frame. Over the stile the trees had formed a natural archway and beyond the stile itself was a lush meadow, where two iron grey horses grazed.

As soon as I saw the stile, I could not help but run to it. This was what I had been looking for, but for what reason I knew not. As I ran I could hear Laurie running to catch up with me. Excitement coursed through me as all my senses breathed in the surroundings, making me aware of my aliveness. As I reached the stile, I turned around and leant breathlessly upon it. No sooner had I done so, than Laurie was there, grabbing my hands and smiling, trying to get his breath back at the same time. "Why did you run off?" He asked between catching his breath.

"Why did you follow me?" I laughed, as I knew he could not stand to be given an indirect answer. He pinched my cheeks teasingly. "C'mon, why?"

"Because I felt like it, I just had an impulse." He kissed me breathlessly and ran his fingers through my hair. As I leant back onto the stile, he pushed his body weight onto me and I could feel his hardness for me, push against my lower torso. I touched my fingertips on his cheeks, encompassing our kiss with the palms of my hands. He pulled back quickly, his eyes sparkling, his face full of a Laurie smile.

"Let's go over the stile, the meadow is beautiful, we can lie down and roll down the slope until we feel sick." He seized my hand, about to pull me over the stile with him, when I heard Katri's voice in the distance, faintly calling.

"Laurie are you with us?" I heard her call.

"They're calling you back. We can't go over the stile, not now anyway." I urged him to stop and slipped my hand from his grasp.

"I can't hear them." He said, looking across to the meadow, as if he really wanted to escape there. "That stile leads to Facric Land, won't you come with me?"

I opened my eyes with a start and was surprised to be enclosed by the canvas walls of the tent because the experience had been so vivid. I could still hear Katri's voice, as I had done in the woods in my mind wanderings. I looked out of my spy hole in the tent's doorway. There I could see Katri, Ned, Kel and Laurie as before, however, Laurie had his eyes closed and Katri was laughing.

"Earth calling Laurie, is there anyone at home?" Laurie then opened his eyes and saw the others giggling at him.

"I was meditating."

"A likely story," laughed Kel.

"Not," put in Ned between sips of coffee.

"I know we had a late night, but that was ridiculous. We were all talking to you and there you were, oblivious to everything." said Katri.

"I was concentrating; you know what it's like when a meditation carries you away, you go deeper and deeper and you block yourself off to outside distractions."

"Too many of those funny cigarettes, if you ask me," said Kel. Laurie stood up and looked across to my tent; I ducked my head instantly, so that I was out of sight.

"I'm going for a walk, 'don't expect to be very long. I've just got to clear the cobwebs away." I heard Laurie say to the others, his voice sounded distant in its meaning, detached. He turned in the direction of our experience; as if to retrace his steps.

"Are you awake yet Jessa?" I heard Katri's voice call from outside the tent doorway. "Because if you are, can you pass me my T-shirt; the sun's getting too hot on my back." I fumbled around among Katri's screwed up heap of clothes and found a pink t-shirt, unzipped the tent and passed it out to her.

"Thanks, I don't know how the boys can bear it all day without their shirts on. My shoulders will be red raw soon, if I don't cover up." She pulled the crumpled looking T-shirt over her head and poked her face into the tent. "You've just missed a funny episode with Laurie; he's on another planet today. We're taking the tents down now; Kel and I have to get back home soon to collect Dylan from his Granny's."

"Of course, I'll be out in a moment when I'm dressed."

"Oh, I thought those were your clothes!" She giggled and leant forward, lowering her voice. "I'm sorry and there I was with the tent door wide open. I'll let you get dressed." She zipped the tent door up, leaving me in the blue glow of sunlight through dark blue canvas; soaking everything with its hue.

My mind raced and spiralled as soon as Katri had left me. Had Laurie really been with me when I had been imagining him? If so, this other dimensional relationship was going deeper than I had expected it to. I had thought that we could only meet one another, when both aware of the others intent and in special circumstances, such as a ritual when both had heightened awareness. If we had been with one another a moment ago, the implications were beginning to dawn on me, for I had only been daydreaming of him. I had had no intention of meeting up with his astral/spirit self then, so did this mean that he could read my mind and I his? Did this also mean that whenever I thought of him, he was really there? Was my mind not my own and could I have the same effect upon his thoughts?

I began to feel a little scared and out of control, as I pulled on my jeans, and tried to locate the remainder of my clothes under Katri's whirlwind of belongings. Was I delving into an experience that I could not handle? How far could this thing go?

I suddenly stopped myself and tried to put everything into perspective. I had no actual proof that I was meeting Laurie in another time. Yes, he had suggested to me on the telephone that this was what was actually happening, but perhaps I had read too much into what he said. As for his eyes being closed at the same time as mine, a moment ago, that surely could have been a coincidence and perhaps he really had been meditating. I reminded myself, that it was not the first time that I had lived in my fantasies and this could just be a delusion. I decided to put all thought of this relationship out of my mind, until it was proved one way or another. I silently put a thought out into the ether to ask for proof of this affair. I then banned myself from any private daydreams about Laurie.

I joined the others to pack our tents and belongings away. Laurie finally arrived back from his walk, just as we were putting the last tent peg in the bag. He seemed his usual self and he paid me no more attention than usual. As we walked through the woods on our way back to the car park Ned blurted; "Jessamyn, we forgot *the Remembering.*"

"The what?" asked Katri turning round to face me.

"I had an *experience* the night of the meeting a few weeks ago, the time we all met Velvet, (although it's nothing do to with her). I hadn't mentioned it to anyone because although I thought it was significant, I didn't think anyone else could make it any clearer."

"But it's been bugging you?" asked Katri, perceptive as usual.

"How can you tell?"

"It's the way of these things. They always bug you until you get to the bottom of them, they're meant to. When you're next at our place you can tell us all about it." said Katri, climbing into their car with Kel and

Laurie. Ned looked slightly disappointed by not having heard all about my *Remembering* experience there and then.

The journey home was a pleasant one and I felt happy to be in the company of Ned. I also felt free for a while of any thoughts of Laurie. I almost convinced myself, that it had all been a charade, concocted by my deluded self to momentarily release me from a marriage that was unfulfilling. I was dropped off at the end of my road and Ned continued on his journey.

At home, I felt exhausted, tiredness swept over me, like a wave. I climbed the stairs wearily and peeled off my clothes, dropping each garment on the floor. As my head hit the pillow, I heard the telephone ring downstairs, and from the office the answer machine clicked on. It would be a message from Michael, no doubt. When we were newly weds, I would have run downstairs to answer it, I would have dropped whatever I was doing. Now I sleepily listened to his voice and there was a final bleep as the machine finished recording. *What on earth is going to become of me?* I thought as I waited for that bleep, then closed my eyes on the world and drifted into a peaceful sleep.

Chapter Four

I Do Believe

'The time, unheeded, sped away,
While love's luxurious pulse beat high,
Beneath thy silver-gleaming ray,
To mark the mutual-kindling eye.'

Robert Burns, The Lament

The week passed by uneventfully and there were a lonely few days. No more was heard from Michael and a spell of quietness had fallen on my fey friends.

Tuesday brought the promise of Michael's return. I had successfully banished from my mind, since the daydream encounter, all mind-wanderings about Laurie. Every time he started to creep into my thoughts, I would imagine him in a box and I would push him down and shut the lid. He didn't seem to mind too much, in fact he didn't seem to mind at all, as he would smile at me each time I shut the lid on him. This disturbed me a little, as it seemed to suggest that he knew something that I didn't. Having him in a box, pleased me and vexed me at the same time. I missed him, but all the same I still hadn't received proof of our supernatural relationship and my doubts grew as each day passed.

The library seemed to smother me, when all I wanted to do, was to be alone with my own thoughts. I was meant to be ordering new picture books for the children's section, but instead I was looking out of the window. It was raining outside and from the upstairs window of the reference library all I could see below me, was a parade of scurrying umbrellas, like a moving patchwork, threading its way along Elgiva Lane. I was transfixed by the moving image outside the window, as if all meaning was lost within it. The summer rain plashed on the grubby window pane. Only feelings trickled through me and I do not know how long I held that image, as rain always seems to make time pass slower for me. Rose, the deputy head librarian, was beginning to turn out the lights.

"The library is closing in five minutes, please collect your belongings." I heard her announce in her broad Scots accent. I knew that I had done literally no work and she would be expecting my book list by Wednesday lunch time. "Jessa, haven't you realised that the library is about to close?" Rose was bearing down over my shoulder and almost made me jump out of my skin.

"Sorry, this list is taking longer than I thought. I'll have to come in early tomorrow and finish it off."

"It really shouldn't have taken you so long."

"I've had constant interruptions this afternoon from readers. I don't seem to have been able to get down to it properly." I lied, and snapping my folder, shut my sparse book list out of her view.

"I see," she brought an envelope out from her cardigan pocket and passed it to me. "A young man came in with this a moment ago. He asked for it to be passed onto you. I did ask him if he wanted to give it to you personally, but he seemed in a hurry."

I took the bulging envelope from her, and saw that where my name was written in Laurie's hand in purple ink, a little crescent moon was drawn after my name.

"I'm locking up now, so you'd better gather your work up."

I clutched the envelope tightly as I scooped up my file and loose papers from the reference desk. Rose watched me, but I pretended not to notice her gaze, as I grabbed my jacket from the office and fled from the reference library. All that time, I had been looking out of the window, when I should have been looking at him. I would have seen him, if I wasn't such a daydreamer.

Rose's eyes burned into my back, as I almost ran down the stairs, stuffing the envelope into my jacket pocket. Once out of the library, I smelled the damp summer air, feeling too scared to open the envelope there and then. I looked down the length of the lane; Laurie was nowhere to be seen and I felt relieved. I didn't feel in the right frame of mind for people, not even Laurie. Brolly-less and sandal-clad, I jumped the puddles along the lane, noticing no one and feeling the trickling rain run down my face. I was heading for the nearby park and once there I ran for the cover of a leafy horse chestnut tree.

I leant my back against the trunk and breathlessly pulled the envelope from my pocket. I looked at it for a moment: the ink that spelled my name was now smudged with the rain water. I turned it over and slowly unpeeled the fold. Instead of a letter, which was what I had expected it to contain, what seemed like a hundred little luminous stars fell before I could catch them. At my feet they lay like a message, written as plain as day on the earth before me.

So this is really happening, I thought, simply staring down at the stars on the grass. *This means that we are real, what has gone before, did happen in the otherworldly realms. This is getting even scarier,* I thought, as I scooped up the stars and dropped them into the envelope.

Once home, I closed the front door behind me and stood on the mat. In the dryness of the house, I realised how wet I was: I had not realised that my clothes and hair were wet through, and now I was steaming silently on the mat. As I stripped the clothes from my body, I felt real in my own intensity. I had to live for the ever now, I just had to do what I wanted to do and live the life of the sensual me. I found the envelope of stars in my suede jacket pocket and seizing it, I ran up the staircase, entirely naked apart from my silver jewellery.

As I ran the bath, I stood on top of the closed lavatory lid and peeled off the paper from each of the stars, sticking them to the bathroom ceiling. By the time the bath tub was full and steaming, the entire ceiling was decorated with luminous stars. I pulled the light cord and plunged the bathroom into darkness. Now my stars shone, illuminating the ceiling and making me smile inside.

As I peered up at the starry ceiling, familiar words streamed through my mind, as I remembered the song lyrics from 'Star of the Sea': *Of on that is so fair and bright, Velud maris stella, Brighter than the dayes light...* (*Fairest and brightest of them all, Even the star of the sea, Brighter even than daylight...*)

This and this only, will be my star of the sea for the next hour, I thought, as I took six candles from a box in the bathroom cabinet, where Michael supposed I kept cotton wool. I placed the candles around the bath, one at each corner, and then the other two, which I placed precariously on an empty soap dish on the loo seat lid.

I stood back to admire my makeshift temple. As I lit my candles I thought to myself that the bathroom seemed magical indeed. I stepped into the warm water and immersed my body. I was going to go wherever the Star of the Sea wished to take me. My starry ceiling winked and sparkled at me, as I closed my eyes, ready for another inner journey, for now I knew that it was not just my body that thought of him.

As I immersed myself, the warm water felt deliciously relaxing. I watched the steamy walls as deep shadows danced from the image of the candle flames. I felt entranced by the fitful fire dancers upon my bathroom walls. The house was beautifully silent, and the only thing that I was aware of, was my watery temple.

Suddenly, my foot that was my anchor propping me up slipped from its hold on the steamy cold tap. Having filled the bath up so deeply, my head was instantly submerged. From the shock of my immersion, I had no time to close my eyes or even to take a breath and once under water, I panicked, grappling with my hands to find a hold on the sides of the bath. The enamel bath was slippery and each time I grabbed a hold and tried to pull myself out of the water, my hands slid clumsily.

At the third attempt at pulling myself out, I realised that I was not holding my breath, however, my lungs were not filling with water either. My hands slipped from the sides of the bath once more, but I did not make a fourth attempt.

Instead, hands by my sides, I began to believe that something magical was happening, and I slipped deeper into the bath, looking up at the starry ceiling through the water. I could not quite believe it myself, but I appeared to be breathing absolutely normally, even though I was completely submerged. This did not make sense, I was scared, but at the same time, I felt excited. A thrill ran through my body, as I felt my breathing going in and out, as though I was above water. I was transcending universal laws and I realised that in these moments I was not of this earth. My body was supposedly there, but the '*I*' that makes the '*me*' was somewhere beyond, '*in*' the present dimension, but not '*of*' it.

I was aware of the water in my ears, producing thick sloshing sounds and a feeling that reminded me of an emotion I could not grasp, filled me. Was it a memory, that I could not define? However, those sensations were the beginning of an awareness that my consciousness was shifting. It was then that reality became blurred and I felt as if I was wandering down a cavernous dream tunnel. I was filled with a profound and dreamlike state of awareness that was pleasant and uncomfortable at the same time, but I certainly did not want to leave it. The water and my immersion in it became the only things that were important.

I began to feel pleasurable sensations, as the beautifully warm water lapped against my skin. It was as if the water was caressing me, lulling me into a blissful state of tranquillity. The water rippling on the back of my hands felt soothing, as if someone was actually running their fingers continually over them, stroking so lightly that it felt seductive. I could not help but glance down at my hands and the sight which met my eyes made me rigid, unable to move a muscle. For stroking the backs of my hands were wispy, stem-like fingers belonging to the captivating body of an elfin woman.

You're the Nixie, I thought as I watched her sitting at the end of the bath concentrating wholly on the act of sensually consuming me. She was utterly naked and her skin glistened with a lustre that could only have been faerie. Her slanting elfin eyes momentarily glanced up at me and she shot me an equally mischievous elfin grin. Her long dark hair, which was strangely like my own, fanned out in the water like feathery black weeds that lapped against the sides of the bath. I knew that I was her willing captive while she did to me with those long beautiful fingers what she wanted, for stroking my hands had just been the beginning. She began to stroke my torso, working slowly downwards and her sensual touch felt like the lapping of waves from the sea over my skin. The experience was all encompassing and I dared not move lest I broke her spell and she vanished.

I succumbed solely to her touch and I belonged to the element of water and to the Nixie. Her delicate fingers moved downwards until they reached my waiting thighs and then deftly stroked my secret place which she caressed lightly, as if these were just whispers of a touch. My thoughts became more and more fluid, as if they were dreamlike rememberings washing into one another. One moment I was concentrating on the Nixie's erotic touch, the next I was reliving *the Remembering,* the next I was with Laurie and it was him touching me and not the Nix. The whole encounter was a melding of mind and body sensations lapping over me, until the one huge wave came, the wave of orgasm. It took me to a place I was becoming familiar with, the place of in-between at the kiss of two worlds. For a moment it was as if my whole existence was suspended and I need not belong anywhere. I glided on the kiss, the moment at which I could enter: where all of experience was expansion of being and moving through space unfettered as an eternal spirit. It was the bliss of blissfulness, until the feelings gradually dissolved and I opened my eyes…

There I found that the Nixie had vanished, as if she had never been there at all. I noticed that I was still breathing normally under the water.

A panicked thought that I was dead, that I had drowned in my own bath water and that all these weird happenings were a death experience, gripped me.

Under the water, I touched my face with my finger tips and grabbed my hair, which floated like tendrils of a sea anemone; I hoped that I would feel my own touch.

Everything felt normal, but the fear of my own death still taunted me. I pushed with the sole of my foot, hard on the end of the bath and managed to thrust my face out of the water. I clutched the side of the bath and pulled myself further to a sitting position, pushing my dripping hair back from my eyes.

I laughed out loud as I touched my whole body, now knowing myself to be truly alive. My body tingled with the sensation of my own vitality. I could not believe what had happened, for I had been under the water for what must have been well over five minutes, never once needing to come up for air. Was it a fluke, I wondered, or could it happen again? For the first time, it had occurred by way of an accident, could it happen if I tried it intentionally?

I suppose, I thought, *there is only one way to find out.* I leant back on the bath and slowly began to slide myself into the water again. I resisted the strong natural urge to hold my breath, as I dipped my head into the water. I felt tense, as I took my first breath. It happened normally. I relaxed my body in relief and slid down further.

This was really happening. I was surpassing the real.

As I looked up through the water at my blurred, starred ceiling, I felt my consciousness begin to shift again, a tripping sensation, akin to eating a potent hash cookie. I felt peaceful and a feeling of never wanting to come back, never wanting to put my feet on the ground, was with me. My mind was swimming in ecstasy, while my body felt hardly to belong to me. I felt as if I was half living in this life, in reality and half in another, in some other time place. It was as though the door was always a little ajar to the other realm, and the other place was leaking into reality.

Soaking in these concepts and sensations, I could have been submerged for twenty minutes or more. I could not tell exactly, for my grip on time slipped from me for a while, as did its container, reality.

Through the water, I could hear a thudding sound, heavily blanketed by the thick, fluid wall. It sounded like footsteps, coming up the stairs and before I could react to this realisation, I saw Michael standing above me, his face indistinct and rippled, as I looked up at him through the water. The instant he set eyes on me, he seized my wrists and pulled me out of the bath, calling my name frantically as he did so. Limp with shock, I went with the moment and allowed myself to be hauled out of the bath. As I was lifted from the water to the normal atmosphere, I felt myself come back to reality and the transition from water to air felt like a journey, as if I had been flying and then I had landed back on earth.

Michael clutched my dripping body to his chest, as I tried to search my mind for an explanation. "Jessa, Jessa," he gasped pulling me closer, soaking through his shirt, making it cling to his torso. "You're breathing, you're all right."

"Of course."

"I thought you were ... you were dead. Your eyes were staring at me through the water as if you weren't there, exactly as if you were dead." He sounded emotional, almost in tears as he separated our bodies, so that our faces were now almost touching one another. He looked into my eyes, his face sad, his eyes searching into my own, as if he would find the answer there. "My God, what the hell were you thinking of? What were you trying to do? I knew you were down Jessa, but nothing as bad as this. I never for one moment thought you'd actually do something like this."

"I wasn't... I mean how did you know I was down, I didn't really know it myself until you said? No, you've got it all wrong, I'm not down at all, just lonely."

"What made you do such a thing? If I hadn't arrived home when I had, I might have been too late, I daren't think about the consequences."

He seemed to be shivering slightly, not from the temperature, but from the strength of his emotions.

"I wasn't drowning, I wasn't trying to...to end it all, only to... escape." I blurted this out, not knowing how to explain, for I did not know what I had been doing myself.

"You would have been dead in a few minutes, if I had not found you. What the fuck's sake were you thinking of?" He shook me, with his hands on my shoulders and then immediately pulled me closer to him again. "I don't know you, do I?" He whispered. "I don't know you at all." I felt sad as he clutched onto my body, as he stroked my saturated hair. How could he understand the truth about what had happened, when it was such a fantastic story? At the same time, I did not want him to carry on believing that he had rescued me from a suicide attempt. It would be easy to leave things as they were, to play the role from his script. However, my conscience would not allow him to be in torment, when what he had really witnessed was my own fascinating experiment in escapism.

He fetched a towel from a hook on the back of the bathroom door and handed it to me, without speaking. I took it silently and wrapped it around myself, as he glanced at the ceiling of stars and then down to my candles. "I'd better change out of these wet clothes, I'll be in the bedroom," he announced solemnly, not even looking at me as he spoke. All this was too much to take in, I certainly had some explaining to do. I wondered why Michael had arrived home so early. I reached into the bath water for the plug. The water was stone cold. I pulled out the plug and retrieved my hand quickly. The water shouldn't have been as cold as that, for I had only been in the bath about thirty minutes and it was very hot when I had first got in it. I looked at my hands and saw to my distress that the skin was very shrivelled, as if I had spent a long time in the water.

Dropping my towel on the bathroom floor, I fled, nude and shivering to the bedroom, where I picked up my big chrome alarm clock: it said 10.35pm.

"Is this the right time?" I asked Michael. I sensed anxiety in my voice as I heard myself ask the question.

"Of course, what's the matter, you look..." I gave him no time to finish his sentence, as I ran to the bathroom, still clutching the clock. I flung open the bathroom door and watched the candle flames guttering in the dim room. They were almost burnt out, they had been virgin candles when I had lit them and now they were just little clumps of melted wax with a small flame, each one burning unsteadily, threatening to extinguish at any moment.

I felt Michael's presence behind me. He took the clock from me, and gently turning me around, he guided me, with his hands on my shoulders into the bedroom. He sat me down on the bed and kneeled before me on the floor, his brown eyes gazing up at me.

"Now please, explain," his voice was constant and steady, his tone was quiet, but I knew it was demanding. "I want to know the truth about tonight. You must have known that I would come home at any moment and discover you. Was this some kind of cry for help?"

"I was in the bath for five hours. I had lost track of time, I didn't know what was going on. I didn't realise how long I had been in there until I looked at the time just now. I didn't even feel the water getting cold."

"What have you taken?"

"Oh please, I'm not into that kind of thing and you know it."

"But some of your weirdo friends are because I've smelt it on your clothes when you've come in. So I can't believe that for a moment. If you weren't trying to drown yourself and you weren't on something, what happened?"

"I don't know."

"Jessa don't do this, I need a straight answer." His voice showed frustration, his caring approach would not last much longer, not unless I came up with a plausible explanation.

"I had an experience."

"What do you mean *an experience*?"

"It's the truth. I fell under the water by accident, my foot slipped on the tap and I went under. Then I realised that I could breathe in the water, as if I was breathing normally."

"You say you were under the water for five hours breathing normally?"

"Yes, more or less five hours. Look at my hands and feet, I look like a prune. I don't know where the time went to; it only seemed like twenty minutes."

"Maybe you believe that you were under that water for five hours, which means you had to have taken something, or all the things that have changed about you recently add up to confirming my theory."

"Your theory being?" I asked wrapping the duvet around my cold body, fearing the worst was yet to come.

"You're depressed or something," he said slowly, not wanting to look into my eyes. "You've been withdrawn; not yourself."

"And?" I asked, wanting to cry, trying not to cry, swallowing, feeling a pain in my throat and behind my eyes. *I will not cry* I told myself as the tears fell down my cheeks. *Damn, damn, damn.*

"I want you to go and see your doctor in the morning; he'll probably give you anti-depressants. It's for the best; you'll be well again very soon." He reached for a tissue, from the bedside table and handed to me.

"You could have told me," he said.

"I told you, I didn't know, I mean, I'm not depressed and anyway this wasn't a suicide attempt, I promise." I blew my nose and stuffed the hanky into the palm of my hand. I dabbed my cheeks as more hot heavy tears rolled effortlessly down them.

"You're not thinking straight. Why don't you go to bed and I'll join you when I've sorted my suitcase out. You'll probably feel better in the morning. We'll start again then." He walked out of the bedroom and I rolled under the duvet; switching out the light, I drifted in a deep sleep.

* * *

I awoke from a dream-less sleep, with the morning sunlight flowing through the white muslin curtains, drenching the room with its presence. Michael seemed to be already half dressed, as he knelt over me on the bed, his tie tickling my bare back, as he kissed me again and again on the nape of the neck.

"What's the time?" I mumbled, barely audible, my face in the pillow.

"It's ten past seven."

"Time enough then," I rolled over, to bring my eyes opposite his, their steady gaze looking into my own.

"I'm really here now," he kissed my forehead, smiling.

"At last."

"I've wanted to feel you all week. Now I can touch you, it feels better than I imagined."

"When did you imagine me?"

"Well, over lunch with a client, in the plane, brushing my teeth, watching the news in my hotel room. Everywhere, all the time, I imagined you, you kept me company."

"In spirit," I said, thinking to myself that my spirit had been in many places in the past week, and with more than one person. Michael sunk from his kneeling position to enfold me in his arms.

"I'm not going away for a while now."

"The house doesn't feel the same without you. I'm glad you're staying, it's about time. You'll never know me and I won't know you, unless we share some time."

"The email might feel a bit neglected though."

"No more love emails, I can cope with that for now."

"Do you ever keep them?"

"Sometimes I print them out."

"Then you throw them away after a while?"

"No."

"So you have a box full of paper somewhere?"

"Yes, I suppose I have. See now you have my confession; I am a hoarder of love emails."

"Why don't I know these little details about you?" Michael stopped still for a moment; he fingered a lock of my hair and then wound it around his finger. He looked as though he was deep in thought.

"Michael?"

"I'm going to be late for work." He kissed me absently and then released himself from our embrace.

"I thought we were going to make love?"

"I didn't realise the time, I've got a breakfast meeting," he said as he pulled his trousers on, his back to me.

I knew that he was keeping his thoughts within and that last night had pressed a button that he had wanted to keep out of reach. Michael dressed silently and left, leaving me with his thoughts. We were falling apart and we both knew it. I had too many closeted thoughts, hidden away in my faerie broom cupboard. He was too much of an individual, finding more empowerment in his separate life. The life he led without me. He lived the real, whereas I only dipped into it: our differences, which were once insignificant and barely recognised, were very present. It was I who had created this situation, for I was the one who had changed. Or was it that I had grown, had searched and had now gone a little too deep for myself? Michael seemed the same as he ever was, walking the same path that we had begun together. It was I who had deviated, I who had seen the glistening, beckoning pool of water at the pathway's edge and jumped in, immersing my whole self. Was I lost without a trace, swimming under the water, barely coming up for air? My questions held no answers and reached no conclusion; I sighed deeply and rolled over onto my front, filling my face with pillow. As I breathed the smell of the clean, bare cotton, the telephone rang on Michael's side of the bed.

"Jessa?"

"Kel." I answered, immediately recognising his hurried voice. "Is there anything wrong?"

"I know I'm calling early, but I need to ring you before I get chock-a-block with clients this morning. Laurie is on his way to me right now, he sounds in a bit of a state actually, which is very unlike him."

"Laurie, what's happened?" I sat myself up in bed attentively.

"I think his girlfriend has kicked him out, it all sounds a bit complicated. He's asked me if he can crash out at my place for a few days."

"It sounds serious then."

"Yeah. I thought he might want some cheering up from his friends, take his mind off it, you know the kind of thing. Katri and I were going to get the Faerie Ring together for a meeting anyway this week, so we may as well do it tonight. Do you want to drop into my place after work, Velvet's coming over too and Ned's already here. He said he's studying, but it looks like a glut of sleep to me. Shall I see you later?"

"Of course, I've got nothing planned, I'll see you later on."

I placed the receiver back gently and wondered what Laurie was feeling at that moment. Did he know that I was thinking of him? I glanced at my big chrome alarm clock and realised that I would have to hurry, or I would be late. I picked up my dressing gown from the bedroom floor and ran into the bathroom; however, I stopped at the doorway, unable to take a step further. The sight was unexpected: I had anticipated the bathroom to be as I had left it the previous night, the starry ceiling and the bath rims, spattered with wax. This would have reminded me, made me believe- that my experience hadn't been a dream. Now it might as well have been, as there was no evidence remaining to prove otherwise. The ceiling was its usual bland self and the bath was completely clean. There was no trace whatsoever of last night's celestial happenings.

For a moment, I wondered if I really was going mad, then my gaze fixed on the cup that was kept on the wash basin: it was over-flowing with Laurie's stars. I felt a sadness saturate me, as I looked at those little stars, and then a feeling of guilt crept inside me too, it was an unexpected shock to feel that way. Michael had tidied away the Laurie stars. This meant that a little bit of Laurie had touched a part of Michael's life directly. This was something that I had not wanted to happen, it was a small connection, but it now meant to me, that Laurie and Michael were no longer separated by a fourth dimension. Laurie was now a real thing in our marriage, and here also, in these stars was the evidence of my affection for another.

I picked up the cup, scooping the loose stars into my hand and took them into the bedroom. Piling them on the bed for a moment, I rummaged through my knicker drawer for the velvet drawstring bag that held my stockings. Finding the bag, I rid it of the stockings, and then stuffed the stars into the bag, pulling the string tightly.

"He must never know, for goodness sake, he must never know, "I muttered under my breath, as I dressed. I wondered how long it had taken Michael to clear up the bathroom, after I had fallen asleep last night. I felt sorry for him, as I watched him in my mind, clearing up after me. It was as if he were tidying up after a child that had gone to bed after a messy bath time game. He was now playing the role of the parent and I the vulnerable child: it never used to be like that between us. Poor Michael, my poor dear Michael, there was so much he didn't know about me, and I the Deceiver carried on helplessly with my guilty games. I had been kidding myself that an affair with Laurie in the Land of Faerie, would be a guilt free trip and that it would be perfectly justified and undetectable. Surely I should have recognised that the unreal in our minds, only mirrors the real in our lives, but in a strange and often coded way. It always seeped through into reality and vice versa eventually, in some form or another. It was only a matter of time.

I slipped on my jacket and stuffed the bag of constellations into the inner pocket. As I wrapped my jacket around me, knowing the chilly morning that awaited me, the pocket of stars rested upon my heart.

The day was just another day at the library and it grew heavier around me, as time went on. I hadn't known what to do with the Laurie stars, and they still sat guiltily in my jacket pocket, hanging in the office. I kept trying to tell myself not to feel so shameful every time my mind wandered towards Laurie. I imagined his hands and the way that they looked so sensitive, I saw his face and his thick, curly dark hair. I visualised him in bits, never as a whole today. In my mind, I listened to his voice and how he was so quietly spoken when he talked to me. *Can you see him, can you picture him? I want you to experience him in the same way that I do; every so often.*

Michael's voice would mix the Laurie pictures, confusing me, for the Michael voice would be so familiar and loving. I felt a loyalty and a deep love for Michael's voice and an involuntary pull towards Laurie's words. I knew that I needed Laurie at this point in my life; he was with me in this other dimensional experience for his own reasons too. I was looking forward to seeing him that night, yet I was scared, as always, of what I would feel for him. The strength of my emotions for him was greater than me and I sometimes felt, they had a will of their own, unheeding of my morals and sensible nature.

"You'll want to finish off now Jessamyn," said Rose, through her expressionless face. "You always seem to be off and away somewhere else and never realising the time. If I weren't to come and tell you we were near the end of the day, I quite fancy, you'd be here until tomorrow."

"You're probably right," I answered as I cleared up my desk. "You're not the first person to remark on it either; I get lost in books." I took my jacket from its hook and felt for the velvet pouch, as I willed Rose to leave me be and get on with closing the library. My willing must have worked, as she noticed a well hidden reader, still loitering in the newspapers section of the reference library.

"The library is now closed. Please follow me and I'll escort you off the premises." Rose left briskly, jangling the keys that hung off her belt as if she was a prison warden. The reader, a flustered looking woman in her fifties gathered her pieces of paper together, on which she had been making notes for well over an hour and swiftly followed the deputy head librarian.

After getting off the bus, I walked to the Wharton's house in a daze, quite unaware of my surroundings, for I was immersed in thought, and didn't care for anything, except what awaited me at the Faerie Ring. My attention kept flickering to mind-pictures of Laurie, as I concocted scenes of him and his girlfriend, Jane, quarrelling. I created Jane's appearance in my imagination, for I didn't know what she looked like. As I saw her, she seemed conventional with short, mousy hair and eyes like a fox's, with a waif-like figure and she was all Laurie's. I had always put the thought of his girlfriend out of my mind. The fact that he had one was in my favour, for that would always keep him neatly linked with someone else. This saved me from being deluded into any idea, that I may ever make something real out of our strange relationship. I assumed that my attachment to Michael served the same purpose for him and so our availability for one another was restricted. That was, until now. If Laurie's problems were really as big as Kel had said, things could end up getting a lot more intense between Laurie and me.

As I turned the corner into the Wharton's street, I saw their terraced house, the face of which was shrouded entirely in deep green ivy. Their house always looked intriguing to me and the thrill I got from seeing it, as I turned that corner, never wore off. The black iron gate screeched as I opened it and walked the short cobbled pathway to their front door, which was ajar as always. I tapped on the door softly, and walked out of the early summer's evening and into the front room. There I was faced with a room full of bright rainbow candles, placed wherever there was a space. Either they had performed a ritual, or one would take place soon. I could hear their voices coming from the back garden. Before I joined them I needed a drink, so I retreated silently to the kitchen.

I slipped my jacket off and hung it over the back of the chair. I could hear soft melodious singing coming from the garden. I sighed with relief, for I knew that I was at home here among my fellow faerie seekers. I forgot my anxieties over Laurie and I simply enjoyed being in their presence. I laid out on the table, six goblets and some slices of honey cake, which I had brought with me. I placed a new candle in a holder and lit it in the centre of the table. I then sat down at the table and listened to the singing, not wanting to interrupt. After a few moments the song ceased and chatter broke out. I heard their voices getting nearer to the house and Ned arrived in the kitchen. He smiled at me and bent over to kiss me on the cheek. "I'm glad you're here," he said.

"So am I. Is Laurie all right?"

"Hard to tell. He's pleased that we're all here anyway; I think it's taking his mind off it a bit." Ned looked around the kitchen. "Wine?" He asked blankly.

"You'll have to open another one by the look of it." As I took a bottle of white wine from the fridge, everyone else gathered in the kitchen. I was greeted by each of my friends with a kiss and a warm embrace. Ned went over to sit on the now clear work surface and Katri leaned against the fridge freezer. Kelsey, Laurie and Velvet, who looked as if she was settling in nicely with the Ring, sat down at the table with me, I noticed that Laurie seemed subdued; his thoughts were keeping him away from us. "I've been thinking about you all today," I said, passing around the honey cakes. "It's been a long day at work."

"How late can you stay?" asked Kel.

"Michael will be home by nine, so I'll have to leave by eight forty five."

"We're all staying the night here," added Velvet, her eyes wide with excitement.

"I don't think I can, I mean ..."

"It's all right Jessa, we know your situation. It would be out of the question to ask you to stay if Michael's around," said Kel, topping my goblet up with wine. "We have a lot of things to discuss that's all, the summer solstice ritual for one. Laurie's going to be staying with us for a while too, as things are so unsettled where he is." I noticed Laurie slip quietly out of the kitchen, then after a few moments I heard his footsteps going up the stairs.

"Am I allowed to know what happened with Laurie, or is it best for him to tell me in his own time?" I asked.

"Jane has broken off their relationship and she's done it in a big way," explained Katri. My chest tightened with her answer and my mouth became uncomfortably dry. I hardly dared ask the reason, but of course I had to know.

"Has Laurie been with someone else?" I tried to sound dispassionate, but I could hear my voice shaking ever so slightly.

"No way- not Laurie."

"Then what?"

"It's a bit more political than that, as far as we're concerned anyway," said

Katri, glancing over at the baby-listener to check for sounds from Dylan.

"She cannot tolerate his involvement in magic. She always knew that he was interested in the subject, but she didn't actually know that he is the Priest of a Faerie Ring, not that she really understands the concept. He had not told her this, precisely because he knew what her reaction would be."

"How did she find out, did he do something bizarre, like talk in his sleep?"

"No, she discovered his Book of Elfin, she read the first couple of pages and made her opinion on that." Katri sipped her wine. "She's sent him packing and changed the locks on their flat."

"That's going a bit far, an over reaction I would say."

"You don't know Jane then. She was in the year below Kelsey at school, he didn't know her well at all, but even then, he hoped he would never have her as his enemy, didn't you?"

Kel nodded knowingly.

"All this makes me shudder. It makes me wonder what would happen if Michael ever found out. He's quite open-minded about things, but he is Mr. Conventional. He likes things to fit into neat boxes. I don't think; 'Oh by the way dear, I forgot to mention it, but I'm a faerie witch,' would go down too well." Katri giggled and slid her back down the fridge freezer, until she was sitting on the kitchen floor. She passed the bottle of wine to Kel, so that he could top everyone's glasses up.

"Times are changing though; it's almost trendy now to be a pagan, especially if you're a teenager. The media are taking a totally different stance from even just five years ago," commented Kel as he handed the bottle back to Katri.

"Mm," I agreed, "but that is because we're aware of every little mention about the occult. Whenever it is on the radio or TV, we prick up our ears and stop whatever we're doing, because it's unusual to hear about it. Anyway, we're involved in it, so we would notice it's every mention. Michael on the other hand, thinks that a pagan is someone who just isn't a Christian. It's not because he's unintelligent, but he just has no interest to find out any more about the subject. Most people misunderstand what a pagan is and they don't even realise that it's a religion."

"Yes, but attitudes will change eventually, it's all becoming more mainstream, we just need a few more years." Kel stood up and cleared away our empty goblets.

"Are you staying for soup Jessa?"

"Please."

"Ned made it earlier, while he was having a guilt trip after having consumed every last drop of beer from our fridge. Then I saw him at the bottom of the garden, with my gardening gloves on, picking great handfuls of nettles." Kel grinned and shot a sideways glance at Ned, who pulled up his sleeves and proudly displayed matching nettle rashes, all the way up his arms. "Oh and there was a fair bit swearing going on too."

"Nettle soup?" Enquired Velvet distastefully, wrinkling up her nose.

"Call yourself a pagan?" said Ned, swinging his legs down from the work top. "You're not a real pagan until you've eaten nettle soup."

"I tried some earlier and it was surprisingly delicious, but of course they were our own, home produced nettles," said Kel.

"Your own home produced wilderness Kel. It's like a jungle at the bottom of your garden, a weed's paradise." Ned lit the gas ring, beneath a huge iron cooking pot.

"Well it doesn't look as if Kel is suffering from food poisoning, so I'll try some," agreed Velvet reluctantly.

Kel took a French stick from the cupboard and began to break it into portions.

"Perhaps you'd ask Laurie if he wants some, would you Jessa? You have a way with him it seems."

"Yes, just give me a moment." I left the cooking smells and slowly made my way up the stairs. I desperately wished that Kel had asked someone else. I felt really awkward talking to Laurie alone, especially after this had happened.

The floorboards creaked on the landing as I walked over them. I knocked on the spare bedroom door and waited for a moment. There was no answer. I knocked again and then heard Laurie's voice come from the bathroom. "I'm in here, who is it?"

"Jessamyn." There was a short pause and then the stripped wooden bathroom door opened and Laurie stepped out onto the landing, closing the door softly behind him. Laurie looked vulnerable and I wanted to kiss him, but I resisted. I couldn't obey my urge, for I was rigid with fear. Laurie hadn't shaved, his hair was tousled and the look in his eyes made me feel distressed. He looked deeply wounded and my heart went out to him.

"You know what happened then?" He asked eventually.

"They thought it would be all right to tell me. I wish I could help, if you need...."

"Don't Jessa, please. I know that you would help, please believe me when I say that I'm not being ungrateful, but words between us like this, are trivial."

"You loved her very much."

"Love. Present tense."

"Sorry, of course you do. What will you do, I mean is it over for good?"

"I'm staying with Kel and Katri, but I don't want to out stay my welcome, they've got Dylan to consider. In a couple of weeks I'll have to find a permanent place. There's loads of legal stuff to sort out as well with the flat. I'm stuck financially until I can sort a few things out. I don't like to admit it, but I'm virtually a kept man, as archaelogists don't earn very much compared to Jane's accountant's salary anyway. So I'm going to have to have to think of an additional way that I can support myself."

"Is there really no chance of getting back together?"

"I don't think so, once Jane has made up her mind about something, that's usually it."

"Katri mentioned that Jane found your Book of Elfin. Have you written anything in there about our experiences?"

"I'm not completely clueless. Don't worry; it wasn't anything to do with you."

"I seem to be saying all the wrong things."

"Sorry, it's just a difficult situation, its okay." Laurie opened the spare bedroom door and gestured for me to enter. He followed behind me and shut the door very deliberately; I knew that he did not want us to be over heard. The room was full of evening light, falling from the large sash windows. The room was quirky, with a low ceiling and a sloping floor. It was a plain room, except for Laurie's clutter invading its usual tranquillity. I stood before the window and looked out at the carthamus-pink sky, spreading like vibrant ink, in-between the sparse clouds. My gaze fell upon the Wharton's wonderfully wild garden and then to the nettles at the very end.

"Nettle soup, - Ned's, do you want some? That's why I'm up here, Kel sent me to see you." I still kept my gaze on the garden.

"Alright." Laurie sat down on the bed. "I want to ask you something Jessamyn?" My heart almost leapt out of my mouth. He had used my full name; it's always trouble when someone begins with your full name. I knew he was going to make us real with his question. I didn't want us to be real; I didn't want to even acknowledge that our relationship existed, not even to him. Now we were alone together and he was going to talk about *us* now because he was single. But I wasn't and this I just couldn't deal with.

"We'd better go down to the others, they'll be waiting," I started towards the door.

"Please Jessamyn. I need to ask you this." He stood up and was gently holding my wrist, persuading me not to flee the room. That was it for me. He had touched me and a feeling like a powerful electric current struck me. I could not have gone any further if I had tried.

"We are real aren't we, I mean us?" I whispered, not daring to look into his face.

"Only to us," he gently guided me around to face him, "only in another place—not here. It's too dangerous in reality."

"Not for you, not anymore."

"But for you Jessamyn. What happened between Jane and I doesn't change us. You would risk too much if I changed our original understanding. I know that. Only if Michael were to leave the scene, would it change things for us." He took his hand from my wrist and sat down on the bed once more. He gestured for me to come and sit next to him, which I did. "Things have been happening to me, ever since we began our... meetings," he said slowly and deliberately, looking into my eyes as he spoke.

"Things?"

"Psychic experiences, strange coincidences," he took my hand in his own. "I need to know what has to happen for you to meet me on the astral. I know we've met during rituals, but there have been other times. Sometimes you just come into my head and then we're off somewhere together, well, you appear to be with me. Are we happening to think of one another at exactly the same time, or are we summoning each other?"

"I'm no succubus."

"And I'm no incubus."

"Well then, sometimes I have just been daydreaming and we meet. When we were on Coombe Hill after the ritual, I was daydreaming then. I didn't mean for it to happen, you took me by surprise."

"Same here, did you have a strange experience last night?"

"Yes, how did you know? I don't know if you're ever going to believe this. I did tell Michael, because it all went weirdly wrong at the end, but that's another story."

"Try me."

"While I was having a bath I discovered that I could breathe under water. I had stuck your stars on the ceiling. I was under that water for five hours, but it only felt like twenty minutes and I saw... I saw the Nix."

"Whoa! That is weird, even weirder when I tell you that something happened to me as well last night. I found a doorway, a way into the otherworld, it was...mind-blowing," he smiled as he spoke. "But hey, where on earth did you go when you were under the water for five hours?"

"I couldn't say. I didn't actually go anywhere, I just felt a heightened sense of awareness, as if I was tripping and then she appeared."

"I can't really explain where I went either. I was sitting in my garden meditating, under my favourite tree. I thought that I had been sitting there for no more than twenty minutes. When I opened my eyes it was dark and Jane was calling me - shouting from the flat. I had been in the garden for about five hours, unaware of the time that had passed." He unclasped our hands and looked down.

"That was when Jane found my Book of Elfin. I never leave it lying around for her to see, I'm always so diligent when it comes to making sure that my magical tools are unseen. However, I had left the book out to write up my meditation, not expecting Jane home until very late; she was out with her boss after work. I thought that my meditation would only take half an hour."

"What were you meditating about?"

"Doorways. It was very strange; there were just doors upon doors. They all led to The Magic Place in the woods and I felt a heightened sense of awareness, as you did. I also felt no desire to come back to reality. It was only Jane calling my name that drew me back. Then we had a confrontation which carried on all night."

"That's the way I came back to reality, Michael was calling my name." There was a short silence as we both reflected. "How long had you and Jane been together?"

"About ten years, but something like this had to happen sooner or later. Secrecy isn't easy; the stress of it gets to me."

"Do you think that the same will happen to Michael and I?"

"Who am I to say? Do you?"

"I don't know what I would wish for, I feel very confused at the moment. Our experiences seem similar though, of the psychic kind. How did you know the same thing had happened to me too?"

"We have been initiated together in the Faerie Priesthood, so we're now sharing a psychic link. We may often know how the other is feeling, so there's your answer. I just had this feeling that something profound had happened to you as well."

"I wonder why, if we both went on the astral at the same time, why we didn't meet up as usual?"

"Did you think of meeting me?"

"No, not then."

"Neither did I. There I think is our answer."

I stood up and walked towards the bedroom door Laurie stayed on the bed, motionless.

"Are you coming down?" I asked, opening the door.

"In a few minutes. I need a few moments to myself that's all." He didn't look at me as he spoke, he just ran his fingers through his hair self consciously.

"Jessamyn?"

"Yes?"

"Would you meet me tonight?" I nodded and smiled inside as I closed the door behind me and went down the stairs into the kitchen, where I could hear Velvet's giggles and Ned's voice.

"Is he coming?" asked Kel, pouring out the wine into glasses on the table.

"He won't be long."

We all settled down at the table and I relaxed. I felt that this was where I belonged, this was my spiritual family. I didn't have to be anyone else except me here; I would be accepted for exactly who I was. Katri raised her glass and grinned,

"Blessed Be," she said as we all chinked glasses.

"Blessed be," we all said in unison. Then we began to discuss our plans for the summer solstice ritual and everyone started to put ideas together.

Laurie appeared at the kitchen doorway, he looked very different from when I had left him upstairs. He had shaved, brushed his hair and changed his clothes. Katri passed him a glass brimming with wine and he sat down smiling, next to Ned.

"I feel a lot better, I'm glad I came here instead of running home to my parent's house."

"So are we, any excuse for a get together," said Kel.

"I wish I could stay," I said "What are you all going to be doing later on anyway?"

"We'll stay up as late as possible, and then we'll probably go out into the garden, lie flat on our backs and giggle about nothing, while we drink Ned's elderflower champagne. We'll do pointless things, like seeing who can count the most stars. Does that sound worth staying for?" Kel passed a huge ladle to Ned, to dish up the soup.

"Not really, I'm glad I'm going home then." I grinned and Kel took a playful swipe at me, I ducked and he got Velvet instead, making us all laugh.

"Oh, so we're not sacrificing a goat tonight or running around naked until sunrise?" smirked Ned as he ladled out the soup.

"According to our neighbours, we do that most nights," answered Kel. Katri began to break up the French bread and as she passed a piece to me she caught my gaze, looking intently.

"Don't think I've forgotten about your *Remembering* experience, because I do get the distinct impression that you want it all quietly overlooked."

"Oh… well it was kind of very deep and personal, but it has been bugging me, and I don't seem to be working it out on my own."

"Well that's why we all work together in a Ring, we're here to help one another. So where do you want to start?"

"I suppose it all began with the Beltaine ritual," I saw Laurie swallow hard and look concerned. *Don't worry I'll edit as I go along Laurie,* I thought to myself. "The ritual that night just blew me away; I've never felt anything like it, the experience really had an impact on me. What I am trying to say is that I believe something really significant happened that night. It was as if a Faerie Door was opened wide to me and ever since I have been feeling catapulted into intense magical experiences, the mother of all of them I have called, or in actual fact I was given the name, *the Remembering.*"

"It's not surprising Jessa, any type of initiation will open an inner door, but of course there are varying degrees of experience in everyone," explained Katri.

"Beltaine is also one of the most potent nights of the year for opening the door to Faerie Land. So that night, along with your initiation would have been an experiential double-whammy for both Laurie and yourself," added Kel. We wouldn't have asked both of you to become the King and Queen of Cobwebs if we hadn't thought you were ready. Things are bound to be intense for a while, but they will settle down."

"So… back to *the Remembering,*" prompted Ned impatiently and everyone laughed at his eagerness, to extract some gossip.

"Well, it happened the evening we had our meeting in the garden under your apple tree. I had been lying on the rug and had closed my eyes and everything began to get distant and dreamlike, I wasn't falling asleep, but I seemed to come out of my body and saw myself lying on the rug. Then a door appeared in the tree trunk and this is where it all got weirder. It was the feelings that I got with the experience that were just as important as what happened. A voice, but it was my own voice said to me, '*this is the Remembering*' and then, to cut a long story short I went through the Faerie Door in my astral body into what I knew to be

Elphame and there I met the King and Queen of the Faeries. I knew then that my life as Jessamyn was an illusion and the real existence was with them. The only message I have worked out is that life is a quest to uncover the forgotten truth about the faeries and, I mustn't keep this to myself."

"Recap, you're a kind of female Jesus with faerie wings and sling-backs then," smirked Ned, whereupon I quickly retaliated by submerging his French bread in his soup. Ned's smile dropped instantly and Velvet and Katri fell about in giggles.

"It is with good reason that sometimes I don't divulge all my magical experiences around here," I said, smiling at Ned's reaction.

"It would seem that life is all a dream," said Laurie seriously, not seeming to notice the silliness of what was going on around him. "The place between the worlds, Elphame is actually what is real and the life we consider to be real – is not."

"Quite the opposite of what we all assume," said Kel.

"That's where the secrets are and the faeries are trying to get us to notice," said Velvet excitedly. "What made me come along to the Faerie Ring was the fact that the fey were trying to make me notice them; they kept hiding things and they would turn up a week later and I was having dreams that seemed more real and vibrant than my real life. I think that not only are the faeries trying to get our attention on a personal level, I believe that they want to awaken humanity as a whole to the lost knowledge, if Jessamyn's *Remembering* is anything to go by."

"It's all getting a bit evangelical with faerie wings for me," said Ned picking up the ladle. "Anyone for more soup?"

"That's because you wouldn't know a spiritual experience if it hit you on the head with a mallet," grinned Katri.

"Steady on, perhaps I have plenty of magical moments, but maybe I keep them all to myself."

"Ned if you ever have a spiritual encounter you will make sure that it will be displayed in neon lights all over London for everyone to see," said Katri. Ned knew that he could not be outdone when it came to Katri, he smiled good-humouredly and attempted to fish out his hunk of French bread with his spoon.

"We'll all think about it Jessa, because if what you're saying in *the Remembering* is right, this is a concern to all of us, not just you." smiled Katri, taking the ladle from Ned and dishing out more soup for everyone.

Laurie looked up at me and smiled broadly across the table, a smile that was meant only for me. His dark eyes lingered on mine and I longed for us to be alone together. That smile had meant that he knew we were on the same spiritual adventure.

* * *

Walking home in the dusky light, along the hedge lined footpath, I relived every part of our evening together. Tonight was the first time that Laurie and I had talked face to face about our relationship and his words; *'only if Michael were to leave the scene, would it change things for us'*, taunted me. I had no intention of leaving Michael, for I knew that I loved him. However, Laurie was now a constant distraction, and my feelings for him seemed more intense.

What should I do about my feelings for Laurie? If I squashed them, they would become repressed, and run like a poison through my body. But having an affair of such an esoteric nature would not harm anyone. A twisty, turny feeling warped through me, as I thought of Laurie.

As I neared my house, my thoughts of Laurie sank deeper and deeper.

Chapter Five

The Deep Red Love Knot

*'...engage the mind-key and part the veil to the
in-between of bliss.'*

The Elfin Eclipse

That night I could not sleep. Earlier that evening, Michael had
arrived home late. He had looked tired and washed out, distant in his
mood and irritable. He did not ask how I was, or what my day had been
like. I was actually glad; it meant that I did not have to lie about where I
had been this evening. After he had eaten, Michael had seemed so tired,
that we had both gone to bed.

*Now you can see me, next to my husband. I am in the darkness, in
company, yet quite, quite alone. See my dreamful husband, lying next to
my guilty mind. His body is outstretched, quiet in sleep. The room is so
full of darkness tonight, for the moon is black, that you may only see our
outlines. Do try to accustom your eyes to the dark air, for I want you to
share with me these moments, as I am nearing a mind place, not within
these walls.*

*Just a short while, and soon I will be there. Follow me won't you
and watch me, if you can in the darkness. The mind place is a droplet,
I'm trying to enter. I have a different way of reaching there, and I
believe it exists on the cusp of an orgasm. The lonely orgasm, easily
sought, quietly and secretly raised, as I lie next to my slumbering man.
As I create my body magic, mine is the bewitchment of ecstasy, seeking
the cone of power to raise my consciousness, to my destination. The wet
moon elixir from my place is my flying ointment on which I ride to meet
my waiting archaeologist. Soon I will be there, soon, soon; just keeping
his image in my mind, just imagine that he is touching my most secret of
places, instead of me. Soon, soon, my body light will guide me, will fly
me, soon, soon, he will enchant me, enchant me.*

"Jessa!" he stands on the bridge of my orgasm and reaches out for me. Reality cusps with the place between two worlds for one second only and that is when I step onto the bridge to meet him. We quickly run off the bridge, for as we look behind us, it dissolves from sight.

Laurie kisses me, a long searching kiss, his dark, heavy curls falling onto my face. Tonight we are connected by more than our bodies. I foolishly believed that because an affair in the astral meant no physical involvement, it would not carry the same weight of emotional entanglement. How could I have been so wrong? This affair carried more emotional complexity than any relationship I had experienced before. We were adding and not taking away to the potency of this affair, because we had given it an extra dimension. This celestial affinity for one another was blowing my mind, as it was not just uniting us in mind, but also in spirit and the spirit is everything, the sum and essence of what we truly are.

He was me and I him, in that kiss we over-lapped and went beyond our boundaries. Our shapes shifted and our bodies mingled in the kiss, the kiss at the cusp of two worlds.

We both opened our eyes and saw that we were in the forest again where we had both first seen the Nix, and we were standing on the banks of the shallow flowing stream. Once again, I was wearing the deep scarlet velvet dress. Laurie was wearing an identical velvet robe, as before. "How did you get here?" I asked him.

"I believe, in the same way as you."

"How can that be? You were waiting for me, how long were you there for?"

"I don't know, seconds, minute's maybe. I can't comprehend the passing of time when I am here. I just arrived at my climax and that's all I know." He looked over towards the stream. "Show me how you breathe under water, as it happened to you in the bath."

"Now?"

"Yes, now, let's do it." I stumbled down the grassy bank and paddled into the shimmering, ice cold water. I hesitatingly lay on my back on the bed of the stream and then gradually lowering my head and face into the water. I held my breath for a moment, forgetting quite how I had gone about it before. Then I relaxed my limbs in the flowing stream and simply began to breathe normally. I could see Laurie's face as I looked up at him through the rippling water. "You look like a nix," I heard his muffled voice say; as I lay motionless, the water caressing my skin as it flowed over me.

Suddenly he was beside me in the water, lying next to me, holding my hand. He looked at me and smiled and I could see that his eyes were smiling too. Most astonishingly, I could see that he was breathing, quite normally. Time passed for us both - silent and surreal. We weren't doing anything except breathing and being. It worked, it filled us up and we desired nothing else whilst in our watery place.

I felt Laurie tapping me on the hand and then he sat up, freeing himself of the water. I sat up too, and as I did, it felt as if I was journeying from one state of consciousness to another. It took me a moment to adjust and then I saw why Laurie had sat up. On the bank of the stream was a woman, aged in her seventies. She was sitting on the mossy slope and totally unaware of our presence, although she was within touching distance. Laurie and I exchanged a puzzled glance, for the woman was muttering to herself and appeared to be looking straight through us, as though we didn't exist. The elderly lady was wearing a thin night dress and looked so frail, that it seemed her skin was clinging to her bones. Laurie stood up and climbed to the opposite bank, to where the woman sat. He picked up a stone and threw it into the water, where it made a resounding plop. The woman looked up, startled by the noise, but she still did not seem to be aware of us. "I'm sorry if we made you jump," said Laurie, but the old woman did not acknowledge his voice.

"Can you hear us?" I asked, standing out of the water and joining Laurie on the bank. The woman again made no reply and did not seem to be able to hear us or see us. Laurie threw another stone, which thudded on to the bank next to her.

"Who's throwing stones?" She asked in a timid Welsh accent and looked startled.

"We are," said Laurie, but again the woman did not hear.

"Perhaps she's hard of hearing?" I suggested.

"She saw and heard the stones, but she didn't see or hear us."

"There's probably a good reason, maybe she's a bit senile." I slid down the bank into the stream and waded over to her. "Hello, do you belong here?" I asked standing right before her.

"Touch her," said Laurie. I went to place my palm on her veined, bony hand, but my hand went straight through. I caught my breath in fright and I swiftly drew my hand away. She seemed to shiver, but she still could not see me.

"I swear someone just walked over my grave," she whispered. Then slowly, with some effort she stood up and walked away. A tree stump was in her pathway, but instead of walking over or around it, she walked through it. She disappeared from view and I turned to face Laurie, who simply looked at me with his mouth wide open.

"This is weird, I can touch you and you can touch me, but I couldn't touch her. It was as if that was her astral body."

"That's it- that was her astral body we saw: either that, or she was dead."

"I can touch you can't I?" I walked over to Laurie and he held me in his arms, our sodden velvet garments clinging heavily to our skin. We both flopped down on the mossy bank and laughed. "That's what happened after I discovered that I could breathe under the bath water. I thought I'd died."

"She must be astral travelling, probably in her sleep."

"What are we doing then?"

"I don't know, because we can both touch one another."

"When we met on the bridge, it was pretty weird, we both merged into one, did you feel that too? What was that, if it wasn't our astral bodies melding together?"

"Well if we're in the place between the worlds, I suppose anything goes. There are going to be people here that are dreaming and others that are astral travelling. There will be all sorts of beings from other realms, like the elementals we saw together a while ago. There maybe people who have passed over. The possibilities are endless."

"How is it that we haven't seen anyone else here before, he who has all the answers?"

"This is our self-made place from our imaginations and deep consciousness. No one else will see the place between the worlds as we do. Perhaps that woman wandered here by accident, she did seem a bit confused."

"We did see the Nixie too, but she's all part of the scenery I suppose, a reflection our higher selves."

"We must be able to touch one another because we believe we can and it's vital for the experience that we wish to have here. Do you think everyone we meet here will be unaware of us though?"

"We'll just have to wait and see, we're only learning the rules as we go along."

"Aren't we breaking the rules, just by being here?" asked Laurie, gently sliding his arms around my waist.

"We're exploring a loop-hole in the rules wouldn't you say?"

"Absolutely," he smiled and kissed me on the lips. The way he looked at me jolted my memory of a time I put away neatly because thinking about it scared me too much.

"Laurie?"

"That's a serious look you're wearing. What's the matter?" He stroked my cheek and I felt that I wanted to cry; it was all getting too much.

"This is going to sound weird, but I need to ask you a question." He looked serious now and stroked my cheek again.

"Okay."

"Do you remember a couple of weeks ago when we were at the Wharton's house for a meeting under the apple tree; the night we all met Velvet?"

"Yeah sure," he nodded.

"Well during the meeting I had to go home and change my clothes and I met you all at The Magic Place much later on. While I was at home Michael arrived and we made love, because I just had to act as normal, I couldn't let on to him that I was only there to change my clothes. The reason I'm telling you this is because I had the weirdest experience I've ever had while Michael and I were making love and I have no explanation for it."

"And…"

"It involves you." There was a long silence when we simply looked into one another's eyes, searching it seemed for all the answers that we had not yet managed to grasp. "That evening at the time I was not with the Faerie Ring did you have an astral encounter, however brief - involving me?"

Laurie plunged his face into his hands and sighed out deeply, running his fingers through his curly dark hair, the way he always did when he was nervous.

"That was when we weren't sure what was really happening between us. It was just after the mind-fuck of the Beltaine ritual. What happened that night Jessa, it blew me away, but at the same time I never knew whether it really happened or not, or whether I was going mad or something like that. In fact it felt so real that I've been almost scared to ask you about it. I didn't want confirmation, because that would have been even scarier." He ran his fingers through his hair once more and his hands were shaking slightly and he could barely look me in the eye.

"That night we all walked to The Magic Place," he began." I think Katri had set up the altar and Ned and I were getting changed into our robes. At that moment I wasn't even thinking about you, that's why it has never been logical, I can't work it out." He managed to look me in the eye; his dark brown eyes meeting mine. "I remember that Ned and I were just chatting about his university course or something. I had taken my shirt off and one minute I was in the woods with the Faerie Ring and the next minute I was in your bed with you and you were…"

"Sitting on top of you completely naked?"

"That would be the one. I even remember looking into your eyes and you looked really surprised, as if you hadn't expected me to be there."

"Which I hadn't."

"Then before I could properly realize what was happening I was back in the woods again and Ned was still talking to me, as you would expect. I remember him asking me if I was okay. I suppose I must have looked shocked or vacant or something, because I just couldn't work out what had happened. I was with you for two, three seconds at the most, but it was a complete experience, like a whole story happening in those few seconds and emotions were bombarding me. If Beltaine was a mind-fuck that experience was an orgy of stuff that was too much for me to handle."

"I apologize, I really do Laurie. You see I can't work out how it all happened either. I didn't know whether it was a hallucination or whether your astral body had actually appeared to me. The thing was I hadn't actually been thinking of you at the precise moments before you appeared. I had been thinking of you generally though while I was with Michael."

"You think of me, while you're making love with your husband?"

"That's a terrible thing to admit isn't it?"

"It happens all the time with married people. Don't be too hard on yourself."

"I don't think that most people think of their lover so much that they accidentally summon them to appear transfigured over their husband do they?"

"Perhaps that is more unusual."

"I didn't summon you on purpose: I wouldn't freak you out for my own gratification. I really don't know how it happened." Laurie paused and looked even more intently into my eyes.

"Did you want me there rather than your husband?" I looked downward instinctively, because I instantly knew the answer.

"That evening I did. I can barely say it; it's such an awful thing to admit to." I looked into his eyes once more. "If you hadn't been thinking of me at the time, then this wasn't a consensual thing. That means that I must have summoned you in some way."

"I suppose so, but accidentally?"

"I swear it wasn't intentional."

"I didn't doubt you Jessamyn, I was just thinking aloud. How can someone have the ability to summon another through time and space unintentionally?"

"I don't know, but it appears that I did and you appeared to me crystal clear, as if your body was with me and Michael had completely disappeared." The moment I said it though I knew the truth, for the answer invaded my whole being so that I could not possibly deny it. I had wanted to be making love to Laurie instead of my husband so desperately in fact, that I had actually wished for his phantom. I had summoned him because of my desire and need for him, although I still did not quite know the mechanics of *how* I had done it, the truth was I had wished him there. I kissed him and cupped my hands around his stubbly cheeks.

"I won't do it again. That's if I can work out how I did it in the first place!"

He laughed and kissed my forehead.

"Just be careful what you wish for," he whispered and I was eternally grateful that he had not been looking at me, because I must have looked startled. It was a moment when I really did wonder if he was hearing my thoughts loud, clear and in Technicolor.

"Don't you ever wonder why?" he asked

"You mean why we're in this together?"

"Yeah, and if it's ever going to end."

"Do you want it to end?" I asked, hoping I knew what the answer was to be.

"No, not at the moment, anyway. We've only just begun the journey, that's the feeling I get. I have a deeper purpose to fulfil by being here and so do you. I am your archaeologist remember and I think

I'm beginning to understand that I uncover things that you don't want to face. You can keep secrets from Michael, but you know that it's not so easy with me. We're in a place where the world has been turned inside out. The only secrets you keep from me are the ones you keep from yourself. That's why I was the one you chose to come here with."

"Then what am I to you?" I asked, feeling amazed at his perception.

"My faerie portal: my key to the Land of Elphame."

"I hope we both find what we're looking for."

"Well at the moment I'm just enjoying looking, whether I find it or not in the end." We both exchanged a kiss and smiled at one another, knowing all the words that we need not say in that smile.

"I feel, I feel light, as if I could float upwards with no effort whatsoever." I giggled.

"Then I'd better hold you down." He laughed putting his arms around my waist. We kissed an absorbing, melding kiss and I felt his fingers run through the tendrils of my long, heavy, wet hair. It was as if he was running his fingers over lengths of seaweed. I visualised my hair being seaweed within the moments of that seashell kiss, on which we feasted. I arched my back and felt a surge of erotic energy course through the length of my body, like a pleasurable electric shock, empowering my essential self. As he ran his finger tips from my throat, over my breasts and stomach, I felt more alive than I have ever felt before. I was in the moment point of now, the place where most power is attainable, the place we were to entwine our potent skin magic. He kissed my stomach through the velvet and he sank to his knees, running his hands over my waiting thighs. I felt him wipe my soft, moist place with a cloth. He looked up and showed me a red handkerchief, streaked with my lunar salve. "A talisman", he said. "To know your scent will be with me always, will mean that I may enter thoughts of you more often." I took the handkerchief from him and tied it around his wrist, tying a deep red knot on his pulse point. He took my hand gently and pulled me down to the soft earth, where I sank my body into his. He lifted my dress and entered me, he filled me up and I felt that now there was some passion left in the world.

Watch us faerie-witchly making love, both un-velveteened now, just our naked skin embracing the live body of the other. Watch us work the spell for aliveness, which only lovers may invoke. Our orgasms, sought in fourth dimensional seclusion.

Through the astral bliss, I heard Michael's voice faintly calling my name. He sounded anguished and there was urgency in his tone. "I'm being called, I have to go," I whispered, not quite daring to disturb our bare skyclad stillness. Laurie, looking sleepy, took my hand in his and stood up, pulling me up with him.

"We may as well leave together. Imagine the bridge Jessa, imagine it with me." I closed my eyes and saw our eclipsing bridge before us, I also heard Michael's voice calling my name again, sounding more distraught this time. I opened my eyes and Laurie led the way onto the waiting bridge. I did not have time to say goodbye to him, because before I knew it, I was lying in bed, as if the astral events had never happened. Michael was calling my name in his sleep, thrashing disturbingly with his arms, flinging the duvet from his body.

I leant over and held his shoulders, in an attempt to calm him, he still flailed in his sleep, as if he was fighting me. One of his thrashing hands suddenly smacked me across the face, with a resounding slap and I was flung back to my own side of the bed. I clutched my stinging face, feeling that I had actually, unbeknown to Michael, deserved that whack. In a numb silence I watched my somnolent husband through the darkness, still writhing and calling my name, in a slurred way, drunk on sleep.

"Michael, please wake up!" Deep was his slumber, for he did not hear me.

"Michael, Michael, wake up!" I called desperately, for I could not bear to witness the scene any longer. He appeared vulnerable, I didn't like him being vulnerable, it scared me. His body stilled suddenly and his eyelids flickered for a moment, then he groaned deeply and opened his eyes fully. He didn't look at me straight away, but looked blankly before him. He blinked and looked at me.

"You woke me up." He said indignantly.

"You were having a nightmare; you were calling my name and flinging your arms about. Look at the duvet if you don't believe me." Michael peered down, where the duvet sat in a dishevelled heap.

"Oh," was all he could utter and he looked hot and pale, even in the darkened room it was apparent.

"Do you want a drink of milk or something?" I asked, climbing off the bed and picking the duvet up.

"Okay then," he leant over and clicked on the bedside lamp. "What's the matter with your face, your cheek is red?"

"Is it? I must have slept on that side. I'm hot, I'll go and get that milk and I think I'll have some too."

I went downstairs in my bare feet, clutching the side of my face where Michael had hit me. The skin burned and stung intensely. I went into the kitchen and filled two mugs with milk and placed them in the microwave to warm.

"Do you want this?" Michael's voice startled me, as I turned around to face him; I thought he had stayed upstairs. He stood in the kitchen doorway, holding my dressing gown. "I made you jump, sorry" he said handing me the gown.

"I thought I was alone, I was deep in thought." I slipped the dressing gown on.

"Thinking about what?" he asked.

"Your dream, you were calling my name. Can you remember what you were dreaming about?"

"Bits of it, we were on holiday together, I can't remember where it was and we were walking along a pathway together and you were holding my hand. We were happy in the dream; it was how it used to be. Then you tripped and fell, I let go of your hand and then you were gone."

"What do you mean gone?"

"It was only a dream. You fell down a well, it looked like a well anyway. I knelt at the edge of it and I was calling your name. I remember that it was an old well and my voice echoed back at me. I could only hear my voice. You never answered back. I had lost you." I put my arms around his neck and we kissed, then he pulled me closer to him.

"I'm here now and I'm not going anywhere," I said, burying my face into his warm skinned, naked chest. The microwave 'peeped' its electronic alarm and broke our spell. Michael took out the mugs and handed me one.

"I feel wide awake, don't you?" he asked.

"I suppose I do. It's three am; shall we go back to bed?" As we both climbed the stairs I wondered if Laurie was wide awake too. I felt guilty every time a thought of him came into my mind, especially when I thought of him in the presence of Michael.

As we both got into bed I tucked my chilly feet underneath his legs. He winced at the shock of my icy feet against his warm flesh.

"You said we were happy in the dream, how it used to be. I know things have changed, I've felt discontented too." He looked up from sipping his milk, his eyes stared into mine, the first time for a long while, that we had looked into each others eyes with honesty.

"You've felt distant from me Jessa; it's as if I don't know you."

"You've always felt as if I'm not letting you in, what can I do about it?"

"Tell me what's going on, talk to me. Let me know your feelings once in a while. You just said it yourself; you're not letting me in."

"What if I let you in and you don't like what you see, or you don't understand, what will happen then?"

"Then I'll just have to get used to it. I married you for better, or for worse. I still love you Jessa, it just feels like there is a brick wall between us."

"You're away so often, we live our own independent lives when you are away. We've even got separate friends. It's difficult to be close. I find myself turning to other people in stressful times, when I would rather be turning to you." I put my mug on the bedside table and wiggled down into the bed, so that I was now looking up at him. He had a kind, soft face, with dark eyes, eyes that sparkled in any light. "I want things to work for us together and I still love you Michael." He smiled as I finished speaking and took another sip from his mug.

"Did you go to the doctor's today?" He asked. I closed my eyes and paused deeply, wishing that he had not asked that question. I swallowed hard and answered a blank.

"No."

"Did you make an appointment? Did you make any attempt at all to see your doctor?" His voice carried a tinge of annoyance. I kept my eyes shut, not daring to look into his eyes.

"No, I haven't and I don't need to. I don't believe I'm ill. What you saw last night was not a suicide attempt. I told you the truth, and you don't believe me."

"How do you expect me to believe a delusion like that? You are lying to yourself. I think you need some help and I'm being caring. You're not making things easy for our relationship Jessa."

I sighed and opened my eyes.

"Just give me some time Michael and it will all fall into place. Let's go to sleep now." I kissed him on the cheek and he simply stared into my eyes. He was staring, but not looking, as if his thoughts were away, far away. It was quite plain to me, that I was the one who was disrupting our marriage. Michael was drifting along, as he had always done, being his constant self. Had I mislead him into marrying someone who I was not? He had an uncomplicated, straight forward nature, asking only the same in return. I wanted to stop the relationship that Laurie and I were conducting guiltily and I certainly didn't want to transfer it to the third dimension. The Land of Faerie was risky enough for me. I felt that I was abusing my privilege of being a Faerie Priestess, by using my abilities to gain access to the astral realms for a sly purpose, and also using the time in which we met at the Ring for our secret other-realm meetings. We really should have been contributing to the Faerie Ring group and its magical workings, although we would not be the first astral lovers to be distracted by a spiritual marriage, as W.B Yates and Maud Gonne had been there well before we had.

However, I felt that Laurie and I were on a route of no return together and if I carried on, I could uncover things about myself and Laurie that had been troubling me for years. I realised that if the other members of the Ring found out about our concealed astral affair, they would feel understandably betrayed and deceived, it might even mean that we would have to leave. It was a case of stopping the affair, stopping the guilt and the deceit now, or carrying on with the journey with Laurie and taking the consequences. How did I know, that if I carried on with it, that it would ever end? It may last the rest of our lives, and if that were the case, it would surely ruin my marriage, and jeopardise any further relationships that Laurie might have too.

Michael blinked, as if waking from a trance and kissed me on the forehead.

"What are you thinking?" he asked, turning out his bedside lamp.

"Thoughts too deep to say." I answered.

"You'll have to catch them in a butterfly net and press them in a book to keep for me. That's the only way I will ever get near to your thoughts Jessa." He turned away from me and I felt that I was overwhelmed by his silence for me. *It's self inflicted,* I thought. *I created his silence and if I carry on this way, secretly loving another and also concealing my true religion from him, he will stop trying to get through to me and then it will be me who cannot get to him. It will be a self-defence mechanism and I know all about those.* I turned over to face his back and I put my arms around his waist, he did not resist my affection. It was not too late to make amends for my foolishness. I resolved, that strange waking night, to put an end to my affair with Laurie and try and work on saving my marriage. It would be possible, if my heart was truly in it.

Chapter Six

Spell of the Nix

*'He's taken her by the milk white hand
And by the grass green sleeve.
He's led her to the fairy ground
And spierd at her nae leave.'*

Anon, Tam Lin

Michael wasn't in bed beside me when I awoke, and dreamily groped the empty pillow. I could hear the beautiful sound of rain, plashing against the window pane and the room was sombrous, appearing sunless. I crept out of bed, leaving its secure warmth behind and I went over to the sash window, where the curtains had already been opened. Michael's pale silver Audi was still parked in the street outside: it 'shouted' *executive* to me whenever I looked at it. I quickly glanced away and as I opened the bedroom door, I could hear his voice talking on the telephone in the hallway below. I could not hear his words distinctly, as I crossed the landing into the bathroom, closing the door behind me. A few moments later, as I was rinsing my hair of shampoo, he opened the door. "I'm off to work now." He said, as I flung a towel over my head. I looked up to see him standing in the doorway, wearing his crisp, white shirt and smelling faintly of soap and aftershave.

"You're going in early?"

"I've got a breakfast meeting with an author who is only in the country for a short time. I was just on the phone to her a moment ago and she wants to meet me in half an hour. I'll have to go now if I want to make it."

"That's a shame. I needed to talk with you this morning, but it can wait. I stayed awake thinking after you fell asleep."

My towel accidentally slipped as I went to kiss him goodbye and it fell from my head to the floor. My sopping wet hair hung around my shoulders and down my bare back, clinging to my skin like fronds of bladder wrack. I watched Michael's eyes suddenly widen and he stood staring at me, as if he was unable to move. "You'd better be going then, if you want to make that meeting." I said. He slowly stretched out a hand and touched my wet hair, as if it was a specimen in a museum. "Michael, what's the matter, you're looking at me so strangely?"

"It's your hair. It reminded me of my dream last night. I had forgotten that when you fell in to the well, I could just see you floating in the water and your hair was fanned out around your face. You looked like a mer ... no not that, something more bewitching. What are they called, the ones that lure men? I think I read about them once...a nix, yes a nix. That's what you looked like for a moment when your wet hair fell down." The word nix stung me as he said it and Laurie's words coursed through my mind. "It was such a clear image, that I don't know why I forgot about it." He kissed my wet cheek, as trickles of water were running down my face from my hair. "That's what you looked like in the bath the other night too. It must have been on my mind, that's why I dreamt about you looking that way." He took his keys from his jacket pocket. "I'll see you tonight then." He kissed me once more on my cheek, as if he wanted to make sure I was real, and then left.

Could Michael have picked up on what was happening to me in the astral realm? Michael had described me, exactly as Laurie had done, as a nix. Perhaps I was making too much of this and it was all a coincidence, but I wondered if Michael could have seen a glimpse of me in the astral, floating in the water? This was all getting sillier by the minute and also more risky, if my assumptions about Michael's dream were correct. I had to stop this liaison now, before I got myself more deeply entwined, if that were possible?

All I had to do, to finish the affair with Laurie, was to stop visualizing him. This was not going to be an easy thing to achieve, for if I squashed Laurie from my thoughts, even though I still truly had feelings for him, he would seep into my dream life. By starting an astral affair, I realized that I had begun the thing most difficult to stop. Ending an affair in the physical, just takes the courage to face the other person and tell them that it's over. However, the astral affair is already tuned in to a higher frequency and so it is almost immune to your conscious actions, only responding to what your higher self desires. For things that go unsaid in the physical, create ripples on the astral. Human beings are communicating on the ether all the time, in our dream states and by our thoughts. It is wise to be careful at what goes unsaid, for it is transmitted, shooting like an arrow from a bow, into the other person's heart.

I realized that I was shivering and I was hungry needing something to fill the emotional gap and take the pain of emptiness away. The house seemed too quiet now that Michael was gone; his presence filled our home more completely than mine. I picked my towel from the floor and wrapped my hair up in it again. I took Michael's dressing gown off the bathroom door and put it on. I wanted to feel something of him around me; I needed to concentrate on the feelings for him that had been submerged within me. I had to feel them all over again. For at the moment I was Mrs. Fawn in body, but not in mind. That part of me was always with someone else. I had to stop living in an unreal place or life would pass me by and I would only have dreamt it away. Dreams are beautiful for themselves, but you cannot live in them too long without paying a price: although I knew that, I did not always live it.

I pulled the silk around my body, as if it were his arms around me and then made myself a hot bowl of porridge running honey into it in spirals of golden, glistening nectar from a teaspoon, held at a height. I had fetched our wedding album while the porridge had been bubbling on the stove and now I sat at the kitchen table, slowly turning over the white pages. Our wedding day was almost four years ago now and Michael had not altered from the photographs, but I had changed. I looked more contented in those photographs, even on the inside, life had been less complicated then. I looked at the circlet of roses in my hair and wished that I could wear flowers in my hair every day; I thought that it would make life seem less banal. That was the trouble with married life; you became mundane to one another as if married people suffer from a glut of love and passion. Marriage partners had overdosed on the sensual sharing of one another, so in the end they become benumbed to the sexual electricity between them. I think it is still there, but it has been smothered by folds of domesticity. You realise the passion has faded when you are washing the crustiest saucepan and he comes up behind you and starts to fondle your breasts. You know that the magic has faded when you nudge him gently away and somehow getting scrambled egg off the saucepan is higher on your list of priorities, than impulsive sex over the kitchen worktop, keeping most of your clothes still on. This was the state that my marriage to Michael had now reached.

When I had finished my breakfast, I purposefully left the photograph album on the table. I had not looked at it for a long time and although I now felt sadness at the married state, it made me feel more involved with my relationship with Michael. I only possessed one photograph of Laurie, it was a blurred picture of him sitting on the grass in the Wharton's garden on a summers evening last year. He was smoking a cigarette and looking relaxed and far away in his thoughts. The photo was in between the pages of my diary, I carried my diary with me in my handbag everywhere I went. I did not carry a photo of Michael with me I thought, as I shut the album. This behaviour was not conducive to ending the affair; I went into the hallway and snatched the picture of Laurie from my diary. I meant to destroy it, but I knew that I could not. Destroying his image would be like erasing him symbolically from my memory. I couldn't tear up his photo and I was, (to my distress) unable to put it back in the diary out of sight.

I felt inextricably connected to him and felt panic at severing my romantic links with him. A Laurie-less life would have been an existence devoid of magic and spirit. I did not want to go back to a time when he was not in my dreams and my waking astral journeys. I felt I had known him before. On meeting him for the first time, he had seemed familiar in a way that I could not define. Continuing my life without him would be like having half of a life and it seemed that Michael fulfilled that physical and emotional part of me and Laurie answered the longing of my spiritual self. No other person in my life made me complete, and Michael could not transcend the physical and emotional. The only way to personal fulfilment, was to have someone who filled the gap that Michael would never be able to fill.

I knew that I should end the affair with Laurie and a part of me dearly wanted to end all the complications. The girl in the wedding photograph had wanted a simple life with Michael, hoping that marriage would be fulfilling - never doubting that it would succeed. It wasn't that Michael had failed me; it was just that I had gone deeper than I had imagined existed at that hopeful point in my life. I had not known of the sensual, spiritual side of me. The nix-self, as she kept appearing to me and strangely to others too.

As I sauntered to work, following the shallow river that ran through the town, my senses seemed to be filled with water as the river ran furiously and the summer rain sent sparkling straws of water. Two ecstatic mallards quacked constantly as I walked past them, quite beside themselves by the presence of so much water. They made me grin as I watched them in their own little duck world, beads of crystal water covering their iridescent feathers. The grin quickly faded as I saw the most disturbing sight. I came to a halt and I could feel myself shivering with the energy of fear. Lying face upwards in the river was a naked faerie woman, the green water weeds rippled entangling with her dark thigh-length hair. Her full, deep-red lips smiled up at me and her moss coloured eyes looked into my own. I knew she was a faerie woman, for her slight body was tapered and as my eyes ran down her legs, where her feet should have been, there was a silvery mist.

As I was experiencing this enchantment the air seemed as thick as honey and time faded, as if I was sleeping and in a dream. She filled my senses and I could look at nothing else. The sounds of the rain and the river seemed to turn into a watery kind of music, as if the elemental was singing to me, charming me into the river with her flowing, water clad body. As I watched her, captivated by her stare, her face began to change as if she were sending me a message through the metamorphosis. Her deep green eyes slanted at the corners, her whole face elongated and her chin and ears grew pointed like those of a pixie. With this she was even more beautiful and bewitching. I took a few steps to bring myself to the rivers edge, wanting more than anything else to be with her under the seductive water. She blinked up at me, her black eyelashes framing her weed green eyes. In that blink, I knew beyond all reason that I was one like her. Not only was I a Priestess, but I was a nixiewitch, a faeriewitch, her spellbinding was colouring my life and my experience at this time in my existence. The Nixie had found in me a human mediator and she was touching my life in the way that only a faerie can.

The Nix slowly raised her hand out of the water. I looked down at her long fingers and noticed that they too were tapering in a fine mist, as if they had dissolved at the ends. I reached my hand out too and was almost touching her when suddenly I heard footsteps. Looking up I saw a frail old woman in a raincoat walking obliviously towards me, her head under a large black umbrella and apparently not looking where she was going. I stepped aside to dodge her, but I was not quick enough and she knocked my shoulder. I felt jolted into reality and knew a deep loss as I looked into the river and saw only pebbles and feathery weeds on the river bed. The spell had been broken, the Nix had gone.

The white haired lady had a kindly face and she looked up apologetically and handed me my felt handbag. I had not realised that I had dropped it in the collision.

"I'm sorry, it's a little wet, but it missed the puddle, could have been worse." She moved her umbrella so that it covered both of us.

"I wasn't looking where I was going. This rain, you wouldn't believe it was June would you? Are you alright, you do look a bit dazed?" She asked, peering into my face with concern.

"I'm fine." I felt awkward and wanted to run away as if I was a child, but instead, to fill the pondering gap said, "Your paper, it went downstream..."

"I won't worry about that, no matter, as long as you're alright."

I felt a decidedly spooky feeling creep up upon me. As the woman walked away from me down the pathway, I was rooted to the spot, unable to move a step. The realization had stolen through me that the woman I had just bumped into was none other than the frail Welsh lady that Laurie and I had encountered when we met in the astral realm last night. The Otherworlds were seeping into my real life and vice versa and it didn't feel comfortable at all. *This was all too weird for words.*

As I began to walk, I realised that I was feeling spaced out after the abrupt end to my nix encounter and I tried to ground myself before anyone noticed that I looked as if I was out of my tree. I ran the short way to the library, jumping over the puddles, feeling as if I was floating on that spacey, trippy feeling. I arrived at the door of the library and as I wiped my feet and breathed the air of normality that only libraries can contain, thick with the wordy thoughts of its dwellers, I reflected that I really was having the oddest, most extraordinary morning that I had ever had and it was only eight forty-five. What else could happen? I did not dare to think on, as Rose peered at me curiously from behind a pile of books on her desk. I decided to ignore her, I wasn't in the mood for a Rose interrogation that morning. I ran up the stone steps, through the staff room, flinging the door open as I did so and into the ladies. I shut the cubicle door behind me and heard Sheila the administrator calling after me. "... and good morning to you too, Jessamyn!"

I leant back on the door and sighed out loud, for at least I was away from people for a few treasured moments. All I could see in my mind was the evocative image of the Nix, looking up at me with her beckoning eyes. It suddenly became clear to me that water was the Nix's magic mirror; her portal from the Land of Faerie in which to enter our realm. I wanted to know what would have happened, if a split second longer had passed and the old lady hadn't barged in on the scene. I was sure that I had been on the brink of a dimension shifting happening. I giggled at the thought and felt that surely now I must be taking myself far too seriously.

I looked down at my sandals, my feet were dirty and wet, and I squeezed my toes up and released them. They squelched. I grinned and remembered the puddles that I had purposefully splashed through. It made me feel free and childlike and not like a librarian. I wondered why the Nix had appeared to me that morning and I still did not feel as if I had come back down to earth. I would have to close my psychic centres. I closed my eyes and visualised my chakras as vibrant sunflowers, each one closing their petals tightly from my crown to my base chakra. As I opened my eyes I felt a lot better, I opened the cubicle door and looked into the mirror above the wash basin. I looked like me, but at the same time I appeared as if I was shining. It was not actually anything physical about me that was glowing, but something emanating from within my being. I blinked my eyes a couple of times to see if it would disappear, but no. Something beautiful had happened that morning at my nix meeting and I felt as if I had been touched by fey. Mind you most of my colleagues at the library would say that I already was sometimes.

Once behind my desk I slid my sandals off and got stuck into the book requests that were very overdue. A shadow cast over my computer screen and I looked over my shoulder, managing to greet Rose with a thin smile. "You got caught in that downpour then. It's only a drizzle now, you picked the wrong time to walk to work obviously. There's been a phone call for you."

"Are you sure, none of my friends get up this early?"

"Katri Wharton, she wants you to call her back this morning. She says you've already got her number." Rose peered over my shoulder at the large amount of request slips on my desk. "Those will take you all morning, even without interruptions from readers." I decided it was best to continue with my ignore Rose policy and got up to go to use the telephone in the staff room.

"I'm making a cup of tea. Rose, do you want one?"

"Two sweeteners then for me and just a splash of milk in the mug with the Rose on it, that's mine."

"I'd never have guessed," I mumbled under my breath as I entered the tranquillity of the staff room. I went to the telephone and dialled Katri's number, she answered the phone immediately and I could hear her little boy singing in the background.

"I'm glad you called Jessa, what time do you have lunch?"

"It'll be one o'clock today; did you want to meet up?"

"It would be nice if you could, I want to have a chat about..." she paused.

"About?" I filled her hesitation.

"It doesn't matter now; I'll come to the library at one then."

The morning passed by quickly, surprisingly enough. I seemed to glide through all my work and even the readers were pleasant and thoughtful enough to trouble Rose with their queries, instead of me.

I felt invisible, and it was good.

At one o'clock a large plastic spider on a piece of elastic arrived on my desk. I looked up and saw its four year old owner smiling at me. "Hello Dylan, your spiders aren't getting any smaller." Dylan was delighted by the distasteful expression on my face and wiggled the arachnid teasingly around my desk. Katri looked tired and harassed, but even then she still managed to look beautiful, her lush black hair framing her face.

"I made up some sandwiches for us to eat in the park. We'll get some peace there, Dylan will play on the adventure playground."

"But it's raining isn't it?"

"It stopped just after ten. Anyone would think you were Rapunzel in her tower up here in the reference library. You never seem to notice the outside world."

"Two differences: Rapunzel had blonde hair and she got rescued by her handsome Prince: no handsome Princes here today." I clicked off the computer screen and put on my jacket, following Katri and Dylan down the stone steps and out of the library, where we were greeted by dazzling sunshine. The pavement was steaming with the sun. Katri seemed quieter than her usual self, as we walked the short pathway to the town park.

Dylan ran to the wooden adventure playground as soon as we were within the park gates. "Don't go where I can't see you!" Katri shouted after him. He was quite uncaring of anything, except his ultimate goal of that moment, the tyre swings. Katri sighed and threw a blanket down on the grass.

"This will do, I can see what he's up to from here at least." She took a large box of sandwiches and a bottle of elderberry wine from her string bag. "This is one of Ned's from last year; I think it's just about ready for drinking. I've got a whole shelf of Ned's brewing at home. I must say, he doesn't do much else, but he's very productive on the domestic side of things, he's always bottling or pickling something or other." She poured out the potion of Ned's deep vermillion magic into two earthenware goblets. The liquid glittered in the sun and I saw the reflection of my face in the wine as I went to drink.

"So Kat, what's been happening?" She passed me a salad sandwich and looked down taking a sip of her wine, as if creating a dramatic pause for effect.

"Something elfinly exciting my darling," she purred grinning at me wickedly.

"Well?" I asked, my eyes lighting up.

"It all started with your *Remembering* experience and last night things took a different turn."

"They did?"

"After you had gone home it was such a lovely evening that we all decided to go out into the garden and sit under the apple tree. We were all just chatting and joking about on the rug. It began with Velvet, you know although she is the youngest and newest one in the Ring, she is the most receptive to the fey, but I'm sure that you've noticed that?" I nodded in agreement.

"Well Velvet happened to be chatting away to Ned and suddenly she stopped mid-sentence and looked as if she had seen a ghost. Then everyone else stopped talking too because we could see that something was up with her. Then Velvet blurted out, 'Guys, I know I'm not the only one who will be able to see this. Look towards the apple tree trunk.' So we all looked and I swear that even Ned saw it." She gulped down her wine, picked up the bottle and gestured it in my direction.

"Any more?"

"No thanks, I won't. I don't want to give Rose a reason for verbally bashing me around the head. Saw what anyway? You're killing me with the suspense, Kat."

"We saw a tiny wooden door, as plain as day, set into the apple tree trunk."

"About six inches high?"

"Yes, of course you have seen it before. So as soon as we all noticed the little door something weird happened to our perception of reality and time. You know that faerie-warping thing it does when you're having an elfin experience? The amazing thing was that it was happening to all of us at once. We know this, because we compared notes afterwards. Then apparently none of us actually went through the little door, but just by realizing that it was there, our whole surroundings changed. It was as if someone had come along with a black board rubber and smudged out our garden and faded in an apple orchard…"

"Oh help."

"Exactly, like you're *Remembering* thingy. It was Laurie who realised as soon as we found ourselves there and he managed to say, 'Jessamyn's *Remembering* place' in a kind of slurred, mumbled voice. We all felt as if we were having some kind of collective, psychedelic trip, but we instantly knew what he had meant."

"I'm starting to feel a bit sick."

"I thought you might. It's all getting a bit freaky isn't it?" I nodded thinking, *and you don't know the half of it.*

"So then things get a bit hazy from here as we all seem to have experienced slightly different events. Although the one consistent element from here on is that the King and Queen of Faerie and their royal court were with us. As far as my experience goes, I was presented before the Faerie King and Queen and they started talking to me, saying that small acts of magic, kindness and devotion from everyone would begin to heal the human predicament and our Earth."

"So in other words, the faeries' mission for us is not to spread their message, but to live our own lives mindfully and look after our own corner of the planet?"

"You got it. The Faerie Queen said to me that they know that we will uncover the lost magic again, but it takes thoughtfulness. It all links to your *remembering*, binding the message together, to create our answer."

"Then what happened?"

"The King and Queen of Faerie and their royal court faded into a mist with the orchard. It was actually very beautiful and I could have watched the mist receding for ages because it was made of sparkling rainbow colours. We all seemed to realise, pretty much at the same time, that we were in the garden again and Velvet was the first to say, 'look, no door!' Then it seemed as if it had been a dream and as if we hadn't all shared the experience, I think I would still think it was a dream too."

"What was everyone else's experience?"

"I think you'll have to ask them individually, it was too mind-blowing to take it all in last night. Strangely, we all slept really deeply and over slept this morning."

Katri pulled out a knife from her bag and grinned. "Cake?"

"You haven't made a chocolate cake have you?" Katri revealed a round biscuit tin and opened the lid for me to peer in. There sitting like a jewel in chocolate heaven was one of Katri's blissful culinary creations. "A large slice please," I answered and she giggled as she sliced three pieces and carefully placed them onto little wooden plates. The thunder of four year old feet was then heard and Dylan landed on the rug, his face beaded with sweat and his eyes only on one thing, the chocolate cake.

That afternoon, back behind my desk I thought about the collective Faerie Ring experience of last night. Thinking about the events was certainly a distraction from ruminating on my own tiresome Laurie thoughts. I was just congratulating myself at not having a single thought about Laurie all afternoon, when I felt a presence at my desk. "Where would the archaeology section be please?" I looked up at the owner of the beautiful voice. It was Laurie.

Immediately my eyes set upon him, my heart filled with feelings that I had been carefully storing away forever. I had never known anyone to have such an overwhelming effect upon me, and in less than a second I admitted defeat to myself.

This man seemed so woven into the fabric of me and the astral tie of my soul, that I fell into his gaze with no resistance, no resistance whatsoever. I was under his spell and now it seemed he was under mine. "I was washing my face this morning and you appeared as an image in the water. You looked like a nix again." He whispered those words, which sent a thrill down my spine.

"Something happened to me this morning too, but I will have to tell you about it later on." I put my pen down and glanced over to see if Rose was otherwise occupied. She was at the photocopier, helping a teenage schoolboy fill out a copyright form. She would be there a few moments longer. "Shouldn't you be at work?"

"I took another day's leave; I want to find a place of my own as soon as possible. Kel and Katri don't need me cluttering up their place: I want to make a definite fresh start. I feel as if I'm in limbo by staying there."

"You sound more positive than you were yesterday."

"I feel it," he paused. "Is that a bruise appearing on your cheek?" I instinctively put my hand to where Michael had whacked me in his sleep and I winced as it felt very tender.

"It could be I suppose."

"What happened?"

"I can't explain now, things got a bit complicated last night, it was an accident, don't worry."

"I've been thinking over a lot of things and..." He paused and looked down for a moment.

"So have I."

"I need to - I mean *we* need to talk things through."

"After I finish here?"

"I'll be waiting for you..." He smiled, and seeing Rose turn around and head for my desk, he started for the door. I heard his footsteps go down the stairs as Rose peered over my desk.

"I have never known anyone have so many visitors in the work place and it's quite unnecessary considering your work load at the moment. Are you still behind with the book requests?" I knew that Rose would love to have an excuse to report me to Sheila, who was well used to having *a little word* with me in her musty office.

Rose and Sheila savoured every little thing that I did wrong at work, as if this was the only way that they would ever have any power. They despised the fact that I might actually have an interesting life outside the confinement of the fusty existence they basked in at the library. This place was their entire world and it held all meaning and focus for them, home life was simply an extension of the library. They were queens of the library realm, and held proud the daily routine of rich tea biscuits, devouring garden books, talking about ladders in their taupe nylon tights and comparing every day how long a flask of tea kept hot enough for it to be enjoyable. I wickedly imagined that up their A-line skirts there were cobwebs so old that the spiders had left long ago. Yes, these were the original priestesses of tea cosy and jam doughnut chat, the eternal spinsters of library-land, who made it obvious to me, that I did not wear the tiara of Princess Librarian to their liking. I did not share their sponge finger world view, for being young was crime enough in their eyes; but to be attractive and popular as well was highly irregular and quite beyond their library code of conduct.

I felt a smile coming on as I looked up at a scornful Rose, standing with her thickly rimmed black spectacles hanging from a black shoelace around her neck, her arms folded, resting on her meagre bust.

"I'm quite on top of the book requests, there's nothing outstanding at all now." I switched off the monitor and handed her a large bundle of request forms, which she took from me ungracefully and held tightly to her cross-your-heart-bra breasts.

"There's plenty to be getting on with tomorrow, so don't think that you can rest on your laurels," she turned to leave me.

"I'm at a book fair tomorrow Rose, so I'll have to hand that over to you." She stopped in her tracks quite suddenly, obviously perturbed by this unwelcome revelation. After a moment of discomposure, she walked slowly into the staffroom, without looking back. If she had looked her evil gaze would surely have killed me in an instant. I ushered the last of the readers out of the reference library and switched off the lights. As I took my jacket down from its hook, I noticed Laurie, sitting outside the main doors. He was sitting on a park bench with a cigarette in one hand and a paperback book in the other. I stood transfixed for a moment at the sight of him and my feelings for him coursed within me, making me feel the nauseous lurch of deep emotion. I sat myself down on a chair and began to sob, intense full sobs which came from the depths of me. Their spontaneity surprised me for I had not realised that I had felt like crying. Now I knew that the sight of him was the small thing that had managed to tip the balance, there was only so many fraught and tangled emotions that one person could keep within. It was logical that after a while the jug of water would just have to over-flow. I had not told a soul of my feelings for Laurie or even my mixed up sentiments concerning my marriage. I had kept it all hidden away in my nixie well of emotions and now they were flowing down my hot cheeks in a watery release. This was too much for me and all at once I wanted to be a little girl at home in my bedroom, in my nice uncomplicated childhood. Here life had flowed in a simple stream of routine, parental love and security. Instead I was a mixed up woman, who did not know my true place in the world, who was rapidly making a complete bodge up of this grown-up love thing.

I pulled a tissue out of my jacket pocket and wiped my eyes. I walked as if in a trance to the ladies' toilets and filled a basin with cold water, I then splashed my cheeks, letting the coldness sting my face and cool my emotions. I looked up at my reflection in the mirror, a little blotchy and watery eyed, but that would have to do. Laurie was waiting patiently for me outside and there was something significant in our meeting today, he needed to talk and so did I. My face in the mirror was doing the shining thing that it had done earlier. So this is how I went to Laurie, a shiny, blotchy, emotional woman, feeling not quite myself, but knowing at the same time that a Faerie Queen was certainly watching over me and although all was complicated and painful, all was right and I was treading the pathway on this earth that I was meant to tread. I was in tune with the motions of the universe and this was all I knew and could trust.

Chapter Seven

Open the Faerie Door

'O thou bright queen, who o'er th'expanse
Now highest reign'st, with boundless sway
Oft has thy silent-marking glance
Obersv'd us, fondly-wand'ring stray!'

Robert Burns, The Lament

I did see something of my fate, as I walked towards Laurie, for he was wearing the deep red love knot upon the pulse point of his wrist. That sight alone assured me that he was as profoundly entwined within this love affair, strangely conducted on the spiritual plane, as myself. I stood over him and touched the love knot and he looked up at me, resting his paperback on his knee.

"This didn't happen in reality Laurie, so why is it tangible?"

"It's a mystery to me too. I woke up this morning and there it was. I can't take it off." He paused. "What I really mean, is that I don't want to take it off." He moved up the bench and made room for me, I sat down beside him, sensing the energy between us prickle, like a shock of static electricity. "Now I know my part in this partnership. It suddenly became really obvious to me this morning, when your image appeared in the water. You looked like a water-nixie again; you were Jessa, but you were altered to appear more elemental. You beckoned to me to become part of you and the water."

"Me - as a nix!" I exclaimed in whispered tones. "About what time did this happen?"

"I know exactly what time this took place, because Kel had an appointment with a client at eight-thirty, so he needed me out of the way. I thought I would have a long soak in the bath, but before I did I had a shave and when I filled up the sink with water; that's when you appeared."

"That's around the time I had my nix vision in the river."

"Your nix vision?"

"It confirmed something that I have said all along. You are my gateway to the faeries, a faerie portal. It seems that you have some special connection with them and you know that I have always sought faerie encounters. I only ever experience the nix connection with you. I never imagined that it would happen to me alone because until I met you, I didn't have psychic experiences, like you do. I always believed that I was too earthy." He stopped speaking abruptly, as if he had said too much. "I must be truthful to you. I did plan to come and see you today and ask that we don't have any more astral meetings together..."

"I had come to the same conclusion, until you walked into the library this afternoon. Part of me wants to stop this, but another part of me, the impulsive, deeper me can't end it, even though the rational and sensible side knows that it's really a very bad idea." I said, not able to look at him.

"I feel like we're betraying the Faerie Ring and staying in the Wharton's house makes it even more apparent. I feel as if I'm going behind their back and it doesn't make me feel good."

"I've been over and over this in my mind and I keep asking myself, are we really doing anything wrong? Then I think of the Wiccan words, 'do what thou wilt, with harm to none', and we aren't hurting anyone at all. There are people who would be hurt, if they were to find out, but at the moment, the only people who we can hurt are ourselves. If Michael found out, he wouldn't believe me anyway, he wouldn't believe that an astral affair was possible. If you can't touch it, its not there as far as he's concerned. I think the others in the Ring would be annoyed and upset though."

"Do you really think so? They all know that my relationship with Jane has ended and that Michael would never share your faerie pathway. Maybe they would see it more sympathetically than you think. Neither of us is with our soul mate."

"Maybe, I always believed I had free will, but now I think that free will belongs to my hidden self. It knows where it is headed and I can only follow obediently. We could agree to stop this relationship at this moment, but it wouldn't stop me thinking of you and that is where the magic of this affair begins, in our imaginations." Laurie stood up and tucked his book underneath his arm; he dropped his cigarette on the pavement and stubbed it out with his foot.

"I'm in too deep Jessa, I can't stop this now. Come on, I'll walk you home and then you can show me the river where you saw her." We began to walk slowly through Lowndes Park in Chesham and then into Church Street, the early evening sunshine with us, the air smelling of cut grass and hot tarmac.

"Michael has seen me as a nix too; he had a dream last night where he saw me in a well. I am beginning to see that what goes unsaid is the most powerful reality of all. We are all living double lives, the one in our waking real lives and the other in our imagination, or our sleeping, astral lives. Except that this seemingly unreal dream world, does seep over into this world and vice versa. Sometimes I think that the astral and dream life is just as real as physical reality, but in its own way, its own knowing way."

We walked in silence for a while, a pleasant, natural peace, each of us quietly absorbing the other's presence. He seemed to be self-absorbed, in a place quite of his own. Church Street was not a busy road, being situated in the old, less frequented part of the town. The sounds that accompanied us were gentle reminders of the real world, a small yappy dog barking in the back garden, the faint hum of traffic from the centre of town, our own footsteps and the odd car driving slowly past, due to the narrowness of the road and the many parked cars on the roadside. When we had reached the end of the road, we continued our way along a public footpath, flanked by a lush meadow either side and the river Chess running through the meadow.

"This is where I saw her." We both stopped at the river side.

I heard the river flowing, its hypnotic rhythms and refreshing sounds which made me want to listen for hours. *If only life would stand still for a few moments* I thought, reflecting upon my busy life, upon the busy world. If only we had time to listen to nature, our lives would be more harmonious with our inner selves. Instead we listen to the outer stimulus of television, traffic and radio. Our preoccupied, lives divorced from the rich web of natural information that lies now forgotten and unheard around us.

"Feeling reflective?" I felt Laurie's touch upon my shoulder.

"I'm feeling mesmerized by the sounds of the river. It almost beckons to me and I would love to know why." I still felt his hand upon my shoulder and I wished that it would stay there forever. "This is where she appeared to me this morning, and I have never had such a magical experience. She was an exquisitely beautiful creature, I don't think that I ever seen anything so enchanting in all my life. There is something else that happened too…I bumped into the old Welsh woman we saw on the astral realm last night" The touch of his hand compared to the astral sensation that I had been used to from him for so long, had a profound effect upon me.

"Seriously, are you sure?"

"Certain."

"Freaky."

He looked into the glistening river, deep in thought.

"What's happening to us Jessamyn? It's as if we're in a real dream together, like we're travelling downstream in a boat, but we have no control over the destination or the course of the journey, we go where the river takes us. There's a faerie hand at work here." Never would I have heard an observation so profound fall from Michael's lips, I mused.

As if released from a spell, I suddenly noticed sounds other than the river again. It was as if the river had filled my all my senses for a short while. It blanked out the real world, making me focus entirely on its simple elemental truth for those moments. As if reluctantly he gently withdrew his hand from my shoulder, as I turned to continue on the path.

"Monday is a full moon and we have no Faerie Ring." He said hesitating. "I wondered if we could draw down the moon together. I want to experience it with you, as my Faerie Priestess?" He stopped and turned to me on the footpath, his face so close to my own that I could feel his breath on my cheeks.

"We've never drawn down the moon together, that's always been Kel and Katri's role. Why don't we?"

"I would like that," I replied. He smiled and I thought for a moment, our eyes were so fixed upon one another, that he might kiss me; however, he turned away and caught my hand in his palm. He squeezed it gently and a pulse of longing rippled through me.

"I had lunch with Katri today and she told me about what happened last night." I said and he laughed.

"You mean *five go mad in Faerie Land?*"

"That's the one. Katri told me about her experience with the Faerie King and Queen, but she said that everyone's was different."

"Mine wasn't like Kat's. It was kind of mind blowing actually…" he hesitated.

"Will you tell me about it?"

He sat down as we entered the woodland footpath, a shortcut to Chesham Bois, he took off his battered leather jacket for me to sit on. He took my hand and gently pulled me to sit next to him.

"I didn't tell any of the others about my experience because I felt as if it would be telling a faerie secret, betraying their trust in me. I know it's alright to tell you though because the meaning involves you."

He took his tobacco tin out of his jacket pocket and with it a little packet of cigarette papers and he began to roll one up methodically. I could see that among the cigarette papers, a number of them had been written on in tiny writing. He picked up one of them to show me.

"This is what the Faerie Queen said to me. I wrote it down after the experience, this was all I had to hand at the time. I just did not want to forget it."

"I saw the King and Queen of Faerie and they were lying together under one of the apple trees," he continued, "only this apple tree was somehow different. There were little lights embedded in the trunk, all the way up, as if there were little people living there. The apples were the reddest, shiniest apples I had ever seen and it was like each one was an orb reflecting another world. The boughs of the tree were hanging with tiny candle lanterns and it so reminded me of..." He paused in thought.

"The apple tree in Kel and Kat's garden?"

"Yes, that's it. This was a celestial version. It's as if the apple tree in the Wharton's garden is an echo of the one in Faerie Land. I saw the King and Queen of Faerie surrounded in a white light that seemed almost blinding and it was a pure light, like angelic light. There were sparkles of light all around them too, as if it were faerie dust floating in the air, but when my eyes adjusted to the light a little better I realized that these sparkles were actually hundreds of faeries surrounding them in an aura of light. There was an overwhelming feeling of love emanating from the scene as if they were being bathed in God's love." I could see that his eyes were beginning to prick with tears and he could not look at me. He finished rolling up his cigarette, put it in his mouth and then lit it with a flick of his lighter. He suddenly shot me a reassuring grin.

"The whole experience felt as if I was party to something very humbling and that ordinarily people would not see it, even people of the Faerie Priesthood because..."

"Because?" I put my hand over his and squeezed it, he squeezed mine back.

"They were making love right in front of me," he took a drag of his cigarette as if that revelation had been hard to make. "Although it wasn't what you would expect it to be. It didn't feel sordid or dirty to be watching them and believe me I could see everything. It felt the most beautiful thing I had ever witnessed, as if I was receiving God's love from their act of love making. Then came the moment when I felt that I would never be the same again. They were both at the point of orgasm and the energy around them became almost unbearably intense. I thought I would not be able to tolerate it any longer. Then it was as if a bubble had been burst and in that instant I found myself as the Faerie King...I was the one making love to the Faerie Queen; it was me." He suddenly looked at me with a concerned expression.

"What's wrong Jessamyn, you've gone pale?"

"That's what happened to me a few weeks ago. I took Velvet to the Magic Place in the woods and we both saw the Faerie King and Queen making love. Only Velvet does not know that at the point of their orgasm, I became the Faerie Queen and it was the Faerie King who was making love to me." We stared into one another's eyes, for a few moments aghast.

"This involves you even more than I thought. Why did you not tell me?

"I have never told anyone. Like you said, I did not want to betray a faerie secret, but it looks as though you're in the secret too."

He took another puff of his cigarette.

"Now you've said that the jigsaw pieces fit together a bit better."

"How so?" I asked and he picked up the cigarette papers that he had scribbled on.

"The Faerie Queen at the point of our orgasm whispered into my ear some words. It sounded like poetry when I heard it and it didn't seem to make much sense, but as soon as we all came out of the experience I wrote it all down, because I knew it would become like a dream and I would forget it if I didn't. This is word-for-word what she said to me. *Faerie Priest, starlit one, receive the starry sex through our climax of a million moonbeams and there I, your Queen of all Faerie will greet you. Accept the cosmic energy, for it embraces love, the key to the universe. The Faerie King and Queen are within you both. This is my gift to you. Blessed Be.*"

"What did she mean '*within you both*'?"

"That is what I've been thinking about all day until you told me your experience just now and then it clicked. When we were initiated as the King and Queen of Cobwebs, we knew from that day on, when we worked together in rituals as Kel and Kat do, that we would be the embodiments of the Faerie King and Queen. Then we are more than the sum of ourselves. It seems clear to me now that we both had similar experiences, interchanging with the Faerie King and Queen at the point of orgasm, to show us that when we make love and also when we are in a circle, we are being drawn together by a divine force. When we are making love, we are not just experiencing one another, but it is a part of the fey King and Queen making love too, because we have invoked that energy. That's what this is all about for us. We are partly so attracted to one another, because of their cosmic, unavoidable attraction to one another. It's like night follows day, we cannot avoid it."

He stubbed out his cigarette in the earth and stood up, holding out his hand for me to take.

"We're never going to be the same again Jessa. It will change us irrevocably, it has to. How can it not?" He pulled me up and I shook his heavy jacket out for him. He squeezed my hand, running his fingers over my bare wrist, sending little waves of longing throughout me.

"I won't come any further Jessa, Michael may see me with you." For that day we had walked all the way home and had not taken the bus for the last stretch, as I usually did.

"He won't be home for ages yet."

"I'll come to the end of the footpath then." He gently dropped my hand and we walked the little way to the end which came out at the turning to my road. "Can I meet you here at the mouth of the footpath at about eight on Monday night? Will you be able to get away?"

"I should think so; he may go out to the pub anyway. I'll ring you on your mobile if there's any problem." He leant forward and kissed me on the right cheek, it was like a kiss that would come from your brother, very proper and reserved, keeping unsaid any emotion. He turned to walk back down the pathway and I watched him walk away from me.

As I entered my house I felt warmth inside, as if I had just drunk hot chocolate. The emotional warmth filled my solar plexus region and the feeling made me smile. I went through to the kitchen, where the only sound was the old clock on the wall, ticking in its comforting way. I habitually put my handbag down on the scrubbed pine kitchen table and at once my gaze rested upon the wedding album which I had left out that morning. The page was open where I had left it, at the photograph of Michael and myself, our arms linked and me smiling the unknowing smile of a bride. The thought of my failure to banish the affair with Laurie, made my inner warmth instantly fade. I was like a dieter, taking each sinful mouthful and saying, 'I'll diet tomorrow, but just one last morsel now, and then I'll start.' Laurie was like the forbidden chocolate gateaux or the sumptuous pecan pie with double cream. I kept on taking that dieter's last portion and then promising myself that I would give up this sinful pleasure - a pleasure wrapped in darkness.

But faeriewitches don't sin.

No, of course not they just play games with their conscience and then hope for the best. It's not as if I believe in a hell to go to, because what really matters is the now. The present is the most important place to be, the only true place of power. I slowly closed the heavy cover of the photograph album, unable to look at the picture any longer, for I had failed once again and sighing a deep sigh, I wished I knew the reason we lived. I wanted to know the point of it all, why we felt guilty, why we strived to better ourselves constantly, why humans are continually trying to cleanse themselves of their emotional waste? Wasn't the point of life just to experience it as fully and completely as you possibly could, to feel as many emotions and have as many experiences as you could cram into one lifetime? As long as you caused no harm to anyone else, be they creature, human or the planet, wasn't it just enough to be here and do your best? I was always asking myself the '*what is the point?*' question and, as usual this time, it got me nowhere but despair.

It was six-thirty in the evening; I could hear the nice children from next door playing badminton in their back garden. I could hear the old man next-door-but-one mowing his lawn and his wife humming as she weeded the garden. In the background the faint rumble of the rush hour traffic from the main road, birds sang and all life carried on outside my house. I wrote on the back of an envelope in my favourite deep purple ink:

Dear Michael – shattered, had a hard day, gone to bed early. Get me up at six darling.

Love Jessa xxx

I propped the envelope up against the jug of lemon yellow roses I had picked about a week ago; a clutch of petals dropped onto the table, but I could not be bothered to throw the flowers away. I went to bed at six-thirty and shut the world out of my reality for the night.

* * *

The following morning Michael was waiting outside for me in our smart silver Audi, which I was hardly ever allowed to drive. I put on the seat belt and he started the ignition.

"Things are going to be better for us from now on, we're going to be good together," he said smiling.

"I want things to get better." I said, switching on the radio as we reached the M25. I did want our relationship to improve, but my voice sounded empty as I spoke to him and only thoughts of Laurie filled that hollow space within me, the spiritual place in me that Michael had never touched. The day at the book fair was a refreshing change from the drudgery of the library. It felt comfortable to be with Michael for a whole day, something we hadn't had for a very long time. Every so often I would grin, as a picture of Rose would come into my mind, imagining her sitting at my desk ploughing through my mountain of work and trying to deal with the reader's enquiries at the same time.

There was really not much for me to do at the fair, except to wander around the publisher's stands and pick up new book lists for the coming year. Michael was the industrious one, seeking out all the literary agents he wanted to speak to, eyeing up what all the other publishers were turning out this year. By the end of the day his diary was full and his briefcase was bulging with glossy leaflets and book lists.

"I'm totally shagged, do you want to go out for dinner? We may as well as we're in town together." said Michael, as he put his diary into his full briefcase at his own publishers stand. Michael's personal assistant, Jenny eyed me up and down as I stood waiting for him. She looked very interested in me, as if I was not at all what she had expected Michael's wife to look like.

"Okay." I answered, feeling uncomfortable under Jenny's prickling stare.

"Do you want to come with us Jen?" He asked putting his fountain pen into his waistcoat pocket. She did not take her eyes from me as she answered him in a soft voice, which I suspected she kept only for him.

"No, but thanks anyway, I wouldn't want to..." Her voice trailed off and she smiled a distinctly fraudulent smile. "I'll see you in the office tomorrow Michael. Good to have met you Jessamyn." Her voice sounded insincere as she continued to stare into my face, Michael quite unaware, snapped his briefcase shut and looked at his wristwatch.

"Have a nice evening then. We'll be off Jen," he turned to me and as we walked away past all the tired publishers, packing away their stands, I was sure I could still feel her gaze upon my back and it made my insides squirm.

"Let's catch a cab to the West End and make an evening of it, we could go for a drink first," he said as we came out of the building.

"Alright, let's do that." I said to him, smiling, suddenly realising how good it was to hear him say that to me. It was as if we weren't married at all, but still just dating and wanting every moment to be full of one another's company, taking every opportunity to be together. He seized my hand as a black cab drew up a little way from where we were standing on the pavement.

"There's one," he said and he ran, pulling me giggling behind him to the cab. "Soho please," he said to the balding driver as we sat down in the cab, gasping and laughing. "I know a good Italian restaurant there, just off Carnaby Street," he said turning to me.

The evening we spent together engaged me again with my marriage. We spoke about our memories, how we first met, our wedding day, our shared passion for literature. There was affection for one another that seemed to be stirred, amongst the stillness in the atmosphere between us at the candlelit table, a softness emerged that had been lost amid Michael's busy work schedule.

"I don't know why we've left it so long to do this," he said sipping his white wine.

"I am always waiting for you Michael, you know that." He looked up at me uncomfortably.

"We forgot how we used to be, we got into a rut of everyday life I suppose." I said trying to smooth it over and ease his discomfort. I knew that he just didn't want to go there.

"Now we've found it again, we mustn't let it go, we must make time for one another. I know that it's very hard with me being away so

112

often, but we'll create time. I even turned my mobile phone off this evening, it's been nice to relax with you and not feel that I'm constantly on call with work." He pushed his chair out a little and leant back. I looked at him and suddenly felt a deep warmth and tenderness and I realised how loved he made me feel. All at once I had the desire to tell him everything. The urge to do this caught me quite by surprise and before I could squabble with myself over this decision to impart all, I heard myself saying the words that I thought I would never declare to him.

"Michael, the things that I have kept hidden from you, the part of me that I don't allow you to see, I have to tell you what it is." My mouth suddenly became dry and I saw that my hands were trembling slightly. He stared at me for a moment with those kindly brown eyes and then sat forward in his seat; he stroked the back of my hand, which rested on the table.

"You may not like it Michael, it may be a mistake me telling you this. It might change everything between us."

"I promised that I would love you for better or for worse Jessa, you know I keep my promises." He smiled and I wished that he wouldn't be so nice about it.

"I want to know all about you Jessa."

"Alright, here goes. You know of my interest in the occult, all the books about the psyche and mysticism?"

"When haven't you got your face in a book?" he laughed.

"Quite, well it's not that I just take a passing interest in the subject. Ever since I was a little girl I've had psychic experiences and things have happened to me that I've had the good sense to keep to myself. I knew that if I told anyone that I'd seen faeries in my garden, dreamt about things that later came to pass, and had communication with the unseen worlds, no one would believe me, least of all my parents who, as you know, think that a brick is a brick and that's all there is to it." Michael leaned forward, intrigued and he had a serious look in his eyes.

"When I was fourteen my Aunt Carol, who is the only one in our family interested in anything remotely psychic, took me along to a local Psychic and Healing fair. There I met with people, who I felt for the first time in my life, knew where I was coming from. I knew that I wanted to be a Priestess, ever since I was small. I felt that when I grew up, I would be one. The problem was, I didn't know any Priestesses and I didn't know how an ordinary girl like me became one either. It wasn't until I was eighteen that I met a Faerie Priest and Priestess at a Faerie and Angel Fair, we later became friends and they taught me everything about faeriecraft. When I was twenty, after I had served an apprenticeship, I joined their Faerie Ring. A Ring is a group of like-minded people who meet together, to celebrate and honour the faeries in the form of ritual." I paused and felt as if something inside me had disappeared, it was a relief and I felt elated. "So there you are, now you know the secret double life that I've been leading. I do believe in faeries and I have devoted my life to them."

"So you're telling me that I've married a Priestess?" Michael looked shocked, as if someone had told him that he was going to have his leg amputated. "Jessamyn, sane people do not believe in faeries. End of subject."

Poor Michael looked lost and confused and the waitress had placed our sorbets before us in silence. We waited for her to retreat before we resumed our hushed conversation, my life's confession that was cleansing me within, purging me with every word that I released.

"The only way I can describe to you how I felt when I knew that I had to become a Priestess, was that it was a calling. Nuns always say that they are called by God into service and it is the same for Priestesses. We get a magical calling from the King and Queen of Faerie and like nuns, once initiated by the faeries themselves we devote our lives to serving the divine. Unlike nuns, we do not shut ourselves away, but live silently and mostly secretly in our mission among ordinary society. Our only law is that we do as we will, as long as we harm none and that seems to cover almost everything as a guide to live your life by."

"So how do you practice this and how come you've been able to keep this a secret from me for so long?"

"You're away so often Michael that it has taken very little deception from me. My life in the Faerie Ring absorbs me totally when you're away, and when you're home, it's only briefly. The Ring does healing magic to help people and to aid our own lives."

"So where's your faerie wings and magic wand Tinkerbell?" We both giggled.

"In the bedroom, away from prying eyes. Do you mind very much?" I asked him, trying to gauge his feelings and he shrugged his shoulders.

"I don't know yet, I don't know enough about it, perhaps I should read a few of your books. I do think that you ought to be sectioned though." He said grinning. "When you said that you wanted to tell me your secret I thought that you were going to say that you were having an affair or that you were really a man who'd had a sex change operation. All sorts of things were flashing through my mind. It doesn't feel real though, you say you're a Faerie Priestess, but until I see you in a pair of wings, I won't believe it totally."

"My antique pine trunk in the bedroom that I always keep locked contains all my magical tools. When we've got the time I'll show you my dresses and my wand and all the things that make me a Priestess."

"And there's nothing else, nothing else in that secretive head of yours that I should know?"

"No. No nothing," I lied. He clasped my hands in his and kissed them both smiling. I felt guiltier for as well as being a closet faeriewitch, I was having an affair too.

Chapter Eight

Initiation by Faerie

'For if you speak word in Elflyn land,
Ye'll ne'er get back to your ain countrie…'

Traditional Scottish Ballad, Thomas the Rhymer

That night I had the most alluring encounter I have ever had in my life. I seemed to fall asleep as soon as I shut my eyes, I had had such an exhausting day, and I do not remember dreaming.

In the depths of night I woke up, as if I had been awoken by someone. That someone was standing at the end of my bed. As I sat up, rubbing the sleep from my eyes, the far wall of my bedroom seemed not to exist any longer: in its place was a meadow at night time, where the erotic waxing moon had stained the grass elusive silver. I could feel the breeze on my face and smell the daisies and buttercups that grew in the meadow. My visitor was the most enchanting creature that I had ever set eyes upon and I knew who she was immediately. She wore summer flowers woven into her waist length, flaxen tresses and her blue eyes glinted in the moonlight. She wore a beautiful white robe that seemed to be made from gossamer. She was, of course, Queen Mab and she held out her hand to me; I took it without thinking. She smiled and passed me a white cloak, made from the softest material that I had ever touched. I threw it over my shoulders and put up the monk-like hood. The air in my bedroom felt like velvet and I was aware that I was perfectly contented and at peace.

I glanced back at the bed and saw Michael deep in slumber and then I gasped aloud as I saw myself next to him, also asleep. It was a disturbing experience, to see myself; and as I watched the girl sleeping close to her husband, I felt that I hardly knew her. Queen Mab took my hand once more and I followed her into the moonlit meadow. Then I recognised it as the one that our Faerie Ring occasionally worked rituals in together at Forty Green near Beaconsfield. She led me to a mound in the centre of the field that I had hardly noticed when I had been there before. There was an opening in the grassy mound and a light like lunar rays shone from the entrance. Standing at the opening was someone I was not surprised to see. Laurie smiled at me and kissed me on the cheek; he also wore a white cloak, similar to my own. I had looked over my shoulder and saw that my bedroom was nowhere to be seen. The meadow was here now in its magical entirety.

Neither Laurie nor I spoke as it seemed that we were so overwhelmed by the whole experience. With the presence of Queen Mab, we simply stood and awaited our orders, which we knew were imminent. She took Laurie's hand and kissed him on the lips, bringing him closer to the entrance of the mound. I realised that the mound was the entrance to Faerie Land and that Laurie was going there with Queen Mab.

"Nixie," she said to me, looking me straight in the eye and catching me quite by surprise: *she was addressing me as 'Nixie'.*

"Would you kindly recite after me, this rhyme, to allow your friend to enter with me?" She then spoke a verse of the most touching poetry I had ever heard and I then related the rhyme to Laurie. Then they turned towards the moon-shining entrance and walked hand in hand into the mound, disappearing from sight after a few moments. I stood at the faerie portal wondering what I was supposed to do; I knew instinctively that I should not follow Queen Mab into the grassy mound. I did not know how to get back to my body in my bed either. Suddenly I felt a warm breath on my hand and turning around I saw a horse that lived in the meadow. He nuzzled my hand, asking for food and I stroked his soft muzzle and his silky black face. He stood resolutely, as if he was guarding the mound and also keeping me company.

"Can you get me in, Nixie?" I gasped and held my heart in shock, turning around quickly to face the unexpected voice. There stood a young man, completely naked, wearing only a silver seven pointed elven star necklace. "Sorry, I didn't mean to make you jump."

"How did you know my name? Well it's not my name, but what I mean is..."

"That's what Queen Mab calls you, so it must be your name, your soul name. She told me that Nixie would let me into the faerie mound." I knew immediately that he needed me to recite the rhyme to him and this was probably what I was here for tonight. It was an honour that I had been chosen for. I recited the rhyme to him and he repeated it after me, he then leant forward and kissed me on the lips. "Thank you and Blessed Be." He said, walking forward into the drenching light of the knoll, a fellow Faerie Priest walking on the astral.

As I watched him disappear from sight I felt someone tap me lightly on the shoulder, I turned around to see a slight and delicate figure of a girl, aged about ten years old.

"What's the rhyme tonight please?" She asked me, blinking her huge limpid brown eyes as she spoke.

"Have you been before then?"

"I've been every month since I was three. The faeries chose me because I used to leave presents for them at the bottom of my garden."

"You're a true faerie-childe then."

"I must be."

"Who is usually here telling the rhymes?"

"It is someone different every time I come. Queen Mab chooses people that she knows will keep the faerie secrets. She says she'll let me do it as soon as I'm old enough, but it's a very responsible job, you must only let the right people in."

"Oh, how will I know, I'm kind of new at this?"

"You just will." The little girl fiddled with a silver bracelet on her wrist and I noticed that she was holding a daisy chain in one hand, with all the buds tightly closed: she saw me looking at it. "It's for Queen Mab. I promised that I would make her one, she likes pretty things." The girl was a gentle child, almost like a faerie herself, with long shining yellow hair, which grew to the middle of her back. She wore a nightdress and pale pink slippers and she rubbed her eyes as if she was tired. "The rhyme?" She asked politely.

"Of course, sorry." I recited the rhyme as before and she said it in her precise way after me. Then she kissed me on the cheek, standing on her tip toes and whispering her thanks she ran swiftly into the entrance, stopping to wave once and then vanishing into the resplendent light.

This began a steady stream of visitors who all needed the pass-rhyme to enter. None of them I recognised, most of them were in their bedclothes or naked and some wore beautiful long dresses or Scottish kilts. The faithful horse stood by me all night and in-between my rhyme recitals he would rest his muzzle affectionately in the palms of my hands. I wondered if he was a horse in his physical body, or if he was a faerie horse? He was trusting and loyal and kept me company in the dark field.

There was only one person who I knew instinctively that I should not enter the knoll. I had been there a long time, many hours and knew that it must be the transition time of dawn very soon. A tall, young man approached me wearing clothes from the 1920's, he looked fairly poor, he was in a shabby suit and he smelled of cigarette smoke. He did not speak to me at all, but simply stopped still when he reached me. He had sorrowful eyes and I knew he was not from this era. He was a wanderer through time. "You're at the wrong place, I can't let you in here I'm afraid." For a moment I thought from his indignant glare, that he was going to just walk straight past me regardless, but after a pause he simply shrugged his shoulders and then, he vanished before me and was nowhere to be seen. I shivered when he went and then heard the first bird of the dawn chorus begin to sing. I must have admitted twenty or more people into the knoll that night, but not a single person had come out. I wondered if they ever came out and I began to feel anxious for Laurie.

I spied the first rays of dawn trickle in through the trees that lay beyond the meadow. As if that was his sign, the horse suddenly sank down heavily on his knees and the rest of his ponderous body followed, eventually he settled down, sitting on the grass with his hooves tucked under his body and his muzzle resting on his forelegs like a cat. In the quiet majestic repose, that only a horse can conjure, he sat dozing in the half-light. I sat down beside him, suddenly quite exhausted, all energy spent. After a moment I rested my wearisome body upon the horse's massive black shoulder.

I must have drifted quickly to sleep, as I began to dream of a heady and sensuous fragrance of flowers. I saw tiny arms and hands, all with sparkling milky white skin, place bundles of flowers all over my body and the horse's, until all but our faces were covered in flora. I did not see the owners of the lovely arms and hands, but an industrious humming of an unfamiliar tune accompanied their actions. I felt completely contented and all I was aware of towards the end of this fey touched dream was my breathing being totally in harmony with the equine creature that was my living pillow. The images took a long time to fade and when at last I opened my eyes, I fancied that I could still smell a remnant of the hoards of flowers that had been around me.

As I awoke to a bright morning, I could hear Michael in the shower. I had sat up in bed and felt slightly dazed from the events of the night before. As I sat up I noticed some muddy footprints left behind from some barefooted person at the side of my bed. I slipped out of bed and placed my foot over the print, they fitted exactly, they were my own. I ran down to the kitchen and fetched a wet cloth and then came upstairs and began scrubbing the mud from the carpet. This was their way of telling me that it had all been real and not a dream. How I had got back in my own bed, I cannot explain and it was not of my doing.

The footprints were finally removed without a trace and I ran downstairs in a flurry, almost tripping over my nightdress. I went into Michael's study and shut the door. I wanted to use the phone in there so that there would be less chance of Michael overhearing me. I dialled the Wharton's number and wondered if they would still be asleep this early on a Saturday morning, Kel answered almost immediately. "Kelsey Wharton speaking," he sounded wide-awake, as if he had been expecting a call.

"Kel, it's me Jessa."

"What's up?"

"Is Laurie with you this morning?"

"He's still in bed; shall I get him to call you back?"

"It's kind of urgent, something faerie happened to us both last night, but in the experience I didn't see him return. I'm worried for his safety, could you check that he's in bed?"

"Oh yeah, I'm on the cordless phone so I'll go and check if you like." I heard muffled sounds of footprints and a door being opened. "No, he's not in his bed Jessa, the bed's been slept in though. Perhaps he's popped to the corner shop to get a paper. I don't think there's any need to worry."

"I'm anxious because of the particular circumstances that we found ourselves in."

"Which were?"

"Queen Mab took him to Faerie Land. I didn't go with him and I didn't see him return. Weird things with time happen there, I don't have to tell you that."

"Queen Mab, you mean she was there?" His voice began to sound intrigued.

"Yes, I'm worried about Laurie." I tried to play the thing down, I had said too much already.

"Well listen, if he's not back by this evening I shall start to worry and I'll ring his ex and his parents and anyone else I can think of. But until then we just have to wait, now don't panic about it. What were you two up to anyway, cavorting about in the dead of night with the Queen of the Faeries?"

"We didn't plan it: Queen Mab woke me up and took me; Laurie was there in the meadow at Forty Green when I arrived. I half expected the rest of the Ring to be there too. He got invited into a Faerie mound, but I wasn't admitted. I waited for him until dawn and then I fell asleep and I found myself back in my bed ten minutes ago."

"He could have come back while you were asleep. Anyway, if he went to Faerie Land surely it would have been his astral body and not his actual person that was missing anyway?"

"Yes, you're right, maybe I'm over reacting. You will ring me when he gets back won't you? I'll keep my mobile on."

"Of course, I'll speak to you later then." As I had put the receiver down, Michael opened the study door.

"Who was that?"

"It was Kelsey, he's in the Faerie Ring I told you about last night." *What the hell,* I thought, *it was all going to come out now.*

"Oh I see, and you didn't want me to hear your conversation, otherwise you wouldn't have taken it in here?" He looked a little annoyed, standing in the doorway.

"I'm sorry, I know how it looks, but it was Faerie Ring business and that is always confidential."

"Even between husband and wife?"

"Most of the time." He made me feel uneasy, as if he was about to interrogate me with difficult questions. His stare faltered and he suddenly softened.

"I'm going to the gym for a while; do you want to go for a drink at lunchtime? There's things we need to talk about aren't there?"

"O.K, I'll see you later then." He walked over to me and kissed me tenderly on the forehead.

"I feel like I'm Peter Pan and you're Tinkerbell with all this talk of faeries" he said with a smirk on his face, I gasped and playfully pushed him towards the door.

"Welcome to my world Michael." He laughed, picked up his car keys from the hall table and went out the front door. I closed the door behind him and leant my back against it, letting out a huge sigh. I had thought that things would get easier if he ever found out that I was a Priestess, but it seemed that they may be getting even more tangled.

It was a drizzly June morning, the house looked very untidy and it needed a good clean from top to bottom, but I really wasn't in the mood for that kind of mundane work today. I decided to have a good long soak in the bath, although it had been my fetch that had been loitering about in a muddy field all night, I still felt grimy and in need of a cleansing and the bath is always the best place to begin. As I lay in the soothing warm water, my mind remained fixed on Laurie. Only a short while ago I had tried to convince myself that only my body thought of him, only my body yearned to be with him and this whole encounter was just a lustful phase that would wear off in time. However, this pointless exercise in lying to myself had now become transparent to me. It was something else that I was dealing with, it could be obsession, love, infatuation, delusion or all of those things put together. All I knew was that whatever my feelings were for Laurie, they were deep and they felt larger than me. It felt as if he was all that mattered, that he complemented my own personality. It felt as if he belonged with me and that my body belonged to him.

Everything he was permeated my very being and took hold of me in a nympholeptic manner. As I lay then wondering where he was, I had to extinguish every thought of ever giving him up. I finally had to be true to my own feelings and admit that I did want him in the real world as well as the place between the worlds. This idea immediately frightened me and the thought of shattering my ordered life of domesticity and financial security by leaving Michael and all that was familiar, made me shudder. Was it because Michael was safe, that I had always shunned thoughts of our parting? Was he the constancy in my life, as a child sees their parent, a source of emotional security? Perhaps I had seen that in Michael when we first met, perhaps that was what I had fallen in love with, the idea of being emotionally nurtured in a safe environment? Was I now growing up and leaving that parent behind or was Laurie just a fantasy of the highest level, where I could elude real life and humdrum reality? Should I really be coming back down to earth and sorting my marriage problems out with Michael? But no, once again the thought of ever giving Laurie up felt even scarier than leaving Michael.

Laurie was now a part of me and I yearned for him with every part of my being. I felt as if we had met to journey in this life together, but also to transcend this life and its confinements. I saw our souls travelling together in many lives to come. This feeling of being astrally tied to

Laurie had been nagging at me for ages, but I had never actually admitted to myself that we might actually be destined for one another forever. Now that I had realised this feeling that I had been secretly obscuring from myself ever since Laurie and I had first met, I'd felt a calmness. Should I explore this possibility? There seemed to be no other way forward, for my real soul mate was Laurie and there could be no other.

The bath water all at once seemed tepid and uncomfortable. I leaned forward and let the plug out and as the water drained away, it was as if the water was my muddied thoughts and I had washed them away, along with the faerie mud. As I was drying myself I heard the telephone ring downstairs, so I flung on my dressing gown and ran to the hallway to pick it up.

"Hi, it's me," said Michael at the other end, there was music playing in the background and I could hear echoed voices.

"Where are you?"

"At the gym of course. Listen, I've just had a call on my 'mobile' from Jenny; there's a contract with an author that's at a crucial stage and it needs going over. Jen needs my help in the office; I know it's Saturday but it's important. We'll have to give that drink a miss - another time, sorry."

"O.K, will you be home later on this evening?"

"Yeah, it shouldn't take me too long. Don't save any dinner for me though, I can't say what my plans will be yet."

"Alright, see you later then."

"Bye Jessa" and he rang off. I suddenly felt guilty as I realised that I was feeling relieved that we would not be able to have the talk he had mentioned earlier. Plan A now ditched, I decided to put Plan B into action and do what I would really like to do with my Saturdays, pay a visit to the woods. Laurie obviously was not back yet as there had been no call from Kel. *What could he be doing, for God's sake what could he be up to, or more to the point what was Queen Mab up to?"* I went into my bedroom and dressed in my favourite blue summer dress, it almost reached down to my ankles. I sat before my dressing table mirror and taking my brush, I began to brush my long dark hair methodically. I knew that I had to look my best to visit the woods.

As you watch me now in my sun-shafted bedroom, you may think it odd, that I should dress up to look my most alluring when going on a solitary visit to the woods. You see a faeriewitch is a vane sort of creature, but with good reason, for she knows that her body is a gift of the Faerie Queen and to keep it well tended, shining and alive, is to recognise her own inner power. Her body is an outer reflection of the inner state. She also knows that her body is the body of the Faerie Goddess, as we are all fragments of the whole, so to look after it well is to honour the Goddess.

After I had finished brushing my hair, I placed in it a beautiful silver clasp, which Katri had given me as my initiation gift. Every time I wore it, I felt as if I was putting my Faerie Priestess hat on. As I had clipped it into place I had a memory, I saw Laurie in the moonlit woods, myself before him on that Beltaine night. He had taken the chaplet of pale yellow roses from my head and placed the silver clasp in my hair. At the time, this act had aroused me sexually, for it had been an act of tenderness and devotion. Kindness and gentleness in a man always had the power to turn me on and Laurie, my beautiful Faerie Priest had been sexually in tune with me that night, being the embodiment of the Faerie King. As I recalled this scene I again felt fleetingly aroused and as I stood up to leave, I caught a glimpse of myself in the mirror, blushing. But then of course, everyone knows that enchantresses are the least virtuous of women, and there was my excuse. *It is ingrained into my being,* I thought as I made my way downstairs to the kitchen, *and I really can't help myself.*

When I got to the kitchen I busied myself with preparing my offering to the fey people. I put a carton of milk, a jar of honey, a spoon and most importantly some cakes into my felt bag, and then I was ready to go.

The local woods were only a short walk away and when I reached them I could hear a few voices within the trees. An elderly man was calling his dog and some children were giggling somewhere in the distance. I climbed over the lichen covered stile and then stood still for a moment and closed my eyes. I breathed in the earthy summer air and that slight smell of leafy summer dampness that you only get in woodland. A small breeze went through my hair and I felt calm and at home now that I was standing at the entrance to the woods. I whispered a short spell to the Faerie King and Queen to ask for protection and also to keep safe my cloak of invisibility.

"Queen Mab, Mistress of my rite,
Keep my magic from other's sight,

Let me meld with the trees around,
Let no one but me, hear a sound.
Shroud of mist envelop my space,
Invisible to all, my magic place.
Blessed Be."

I imagined a gossamer cloak fall around my shoulders, sparkling with dew drops it fell right down to my toes. This cloak of invisibility, (something that I had used every time that I worked alone in a public place, especially during daylight), kept me from being seen. The cloak of invisibility, although not actually rendering the Priestess invisible, keeps her from being noticed. Walkers happen to take an alternative route, dogs dig up sticks elsewhere and children find that playing somewhere different today, is more fascinating. I have never once had the *cloak* fail me for I have worked rituals in broad daylight in woodlands, right next to a golf course and also in a town park and I have never been observed yet.

I knew where I was heading as I walked off the public footpath and onto the ivy covered pathway that led to *The Magic Place*. After a few moments I spied the copse I was heading to and fond memories stirred. I entered the copse, which was a secluded circle of trees with logs in between the trunks which we used as seats. There were two moss covered tree stumps in the centre which made our altar. It was the most perfect, natural site for rituals and when Kel and Katri had first come across it, it was as if they had been welcomed there by the trees themselves. I knelt before the altar on the spongy woodland earth and took the slices of cake out of my bag placing them on the mossy velvet altar.

"This is for you Queen Mab and this milk and honey too, I know you like them very well." I had placed all my offerings on the altar and I had spooned the honey into a large stone that had a well in it. I had made a cup out of some bark that I wrapped around into a cone shape, to pour the milk into. Then I sat back on my heels and closed my eyes with a sigh. For sometimes I reflected that working for the faeries was not all it was cracked up to be, but then they had the most magical surprises, this I had to hold onto. *Expect magic and it will happen,* I thought.

"You know that I am here faeries, I've come to escape from that harsh world and be with you, if only for a little while. This world has too many sharp edges for me and I never quite get the hang of it, do I? I'm feeling squashed by reality and all the problems that go with it, this life is crushing me with its conformities and stifling situations. I feel that I am somewhere in between the two worlds, but never really gaining the whole benefit of either. As your Priestess, I feel that I am too sensitive for this life, but equally too encumbered for your world. I know that I am privileged to serve you and to have experiences of you, but it makes my life more complicated. You know all this already, this I understand, for it is all part of the journey."

"I've come to you with the Laurie problem, my heart is so torn, unsettled. I am in such pain, emotional pain, as if my body is imbued with it constantly, and I cannot know release. Although I am hurting, I don't want to hurt anyone else, but it seems inevitable that someone will end up being wounded. But to live a lie is a profound crime and the person who exists for me on the deepest level that a human being can experience, has to be the one who is more real than anything else. And now I am in too intensely to go back. I began something that I thought would be a lighter option on the love spectrum and instead, I have discovered exactly the opposite."

"Dearest Mab, don't hold my Laurie for longer than you need, please return him or I will surely go mad. He does not know the depth of my affection for him, he cannot know it, we only meet as playful lovers and always part as friends. I am inextricably linked to him and as yet he does not know it. Laurie come back, I'm calling you. I can't go back to the way I was, you've changed everything." I began to whisper his name slowly, it just came from me as if I was not directing it, as if it was flowing through me, but not originating from me. As I whispered his name, it brought comfort to me and that was what triggered my release. I covered my face with my hands and caught the tears that had begun to slip easily down my cheeks. After a while a sense of inner calm began to seep from within me and I knew that I had cleansed myself. A peaceful feeling came over me and I dried my tears, knowing that this moment was the stillness, the moment to collect within me my own strength and fortitude, a lull in the storm before everything would go haywire in my life. And for this I needed courage, because I didn't even know if Laurie had the same feelings for me as I had for him. However, the words, 'if only Michael were to leave the scene, would it change things for us', stayed in my mind and this I clung onto, my glimmer of hope.

"Queen Mab, are you there?" I knew that she was there, because immediately I had asked the question I had an impulse to go straight to the Wharton's house. I knew that I just had to be there.

Chapter Nine

Mab the Rhymer

'He heard, he saw, he knew too well
The secrets of your fairy clan,
You stole from him the haunted dell,
... would that he might return and tell
of his mysterious company!'

Andrew Lang, The Fairy Minister

As usual the Wharton's door was slightly ajar; I had given a gentle knock and stepped inside. Kel had appeared from the kitchen and smiling he had kissed me on the cheek."I've been trying to ring you for most of the morning, where have you been?"

"To the Magic Place. I just needed some time on my own: I didn't realise I'd been very long. Is he back?"

"He walked in the door at about ten thirty, looking like a down-and-out. Anyway, I'll let him tell you all about it." Kel pushed open the kitchen door and there I saw Laurie sitting at the pine table, with a large glass of wine in his hands. He smiled when he saw me and I went over to kiss him. The kiss made my insides lurch with desire, a feeling so strong within me that I felt slightly sick. We exchanged a knowing glance and he put his hand fleetingly over mine on the table.

"You needn't have worried, Queen Mab didn't do a Rev. Robert Kirk on me and I haven't been a victim of faerie entrapment or anything sinister like that, but I must say that I am glad to be back, so thank you for your concern. We knew you'd turn up here sooner or later, in fact we were so sure of it, Kel got some of Ned's soup out of the freezer and opened a bottle of wine to celebrate my return, so that we could all have lunch together." Kel handed me a glass of wine and we all clinked glasses.

"You will stay for lunch, won't you Jessa?" asked Kel, beginning to break up a stick of French bread and place the pieces in the basket.

"Yes I will, that's just what I need." I sat down at the table and Laurie lowered his eyes and looked seriously into his glass of wine. I noticed that he was still wearing the red love knot around his wrist, as he ran his fingers through his dark curls.

"Do you know what brought me back?" he said taking another sip of wine. I shook my head and placed my glass down on the table. "I heard someone chanting my name and it was as if I was being summoned to leave the faerie revel. I didn't want to leave, I really didn't, there was so much there that I could learn, but I think that I had faerie glamour before my eyes. I didn't care what time it was and even when all the visitors left I wanted to stay, no one mentioned that I should leave. But the voice chanting my name was pulling me back to the real world and I knew that I must follow it. It was as if the voice was a magnet and I was the helpless piece of metal being drawn towards it." There was a knock at the front door and Kel left the room to see who it was.

"It was your voice wasn't it, you were calling me back?"

"I couldn't help it, but I didn't realise that it would actually work. The chanting just happened as if I was being directed to do it." Kel walked back into the room with his tea towel slung over his shoulder, followed by Ned, who had the charismatic Ned grin upon his face. He slapped Laurie on the back and then kissed me and sat down at the table with us.

"That's my soup I can smell cooking Kelsey."

"You're not mistaken and are you here for lunch like the rest of them?"

"Need you ask?"

"No, I don't suppose I do," answered Kel handing him a glass of wine. Ned got a tobacco tin out of his pocket and began to roll a cigarette; he then offered it to Laurie who took it smiling. Ned lit a match and lit the roll-up for him and then he began to roll another one for himself.

"Ned knows about last night, he happened to ring up just as Laurie came back." Kel explained to me as he ladled the soup into earthenware bowls.

"Jessa, were you there all night?" asked Laurie.

"Until dawn. I fell asleep at dawn in the field and then woke up to find myself in my own bed. It could have all been a dream, if it wasn't for some muddy footprints I found on my bedroom floor this morning."

"Laurie said you had to recite a rhyme, what was that all about?" asked Ned lighting up his own cigarette.

"Oh well, I can remember that, I had to stand there all night and say it, I lost count to how many people. The words were so beautiful, the most touching words I have ever heard, it went..." I went to recite the rhyme, but the words would not come out.

"Hold on I'm sure I can remember them, they were..." Again I tried to recall the verse but the words would not come to me, it was as if they had been blotted from my memory.

"I can't remember them, but that's ridiculous, it was only last night. Something weird has happened here."

"What wouldn't I do to get hold of those words? Are you sure you've forgotten, try once more," said Ned. I paused for a moment and sighed in defeat.

"No sorry, they've gone from my head, how peculiar this is."

"Mab's automatic security system I expect," said Kel, placing a bowl of steaming watercress soup before me. "Katri and Velvet should be here in half an hour. I thought it would be good to take advantage of the fact that we're all together, so we could have a meeting to plan the Summer Solstice ritual."

"Is Laurie up to it, I mean have you got your feet back on the ground yet?" asked Ned, buttering his French bread.

"Kel went through some grounding exercises with me when I got back. I feel more stupid than anything else, I broke all the rules in the book when it comes down to visiting Mab's realm, and I even drank the wine. I'm lucky to be back at all really."

"Faeriewitches have sometimes been known to bend the rules in the Land of Elphame, only sometimes, mind," said Kel.

"We're all a little bit fey here, we belong a small way in their world." I said.

"That doesn't mean we should out stay our welcome though," added Ned and we all laughed including Laurie who thumped his forehead with his palm in jest at the remark.

"So next time you both go on an astral expedition to Faerie Land, can the rest of the Ring come too?" Ned added with a suspicious tone in his voice. Laurie shot me a worried sideways glance and I didn't know how to answer the pertinent comment, there had been a momentary silence.

"This always happens in magical groups," began Kel and I almost breathed a sigh of relief, but stopped myself in time.

"You often get partnerships that naturally develop between faerie seekers. The psychic link just clicks between certain people and then all sorts of astral events can happen. Jessa and Laurie are probably on the same wave length, as the phrase goes. That's what happens when a Faerie Ring becomes established, psychic partnerships become very evident. As they are both working together as the King and Queen of Cobwebs this makes this kind of relationship even more likely." I wished Kel would get off the subject very soon.

Ned looked down and pondered his soup. Being the newest member of the Ring, having only joined six months ago, Kel was still often putting him straight on certain matters. However, the fact was that Ned had smelled a rat about Laurie and I and as he was a very perceptive person, I was surprised it had taken him this long. I think if I had heard of two seekers having an astral experience together, I may have felt a tinge of suspicion too.

"So will you be going back there in a hurry?" asked Kel as he handed Laurie the peppermill.

"Well, not by choice anyway. I hope that I've learnt something from the experience. Having said that, if Mab did appear in my bedroom again, with an invitation to another of her heathen revels, I don't think I could refuse her."

"Just be careful not to fall in love with any beautiful faerie women Laurie. We definitely wouldn't see you again if that were to happen," said Ned.

"No chance of that, there are enough faerie enchantresses in this world for this mortal man."

"Oh yes?" said Ned raising his eyebrows.

"Yes, and make sure you don't fall under their spell when you meet one. It's fatal and then you might as well live in Faerie Land,"

"You sound like someone who speaks from experience Laurie?" asked Ned seemingly more intrigued.

"No of course not, it's just something Kel talked about in our training sessions when I was his apprentice. You see, that's where Katri comes in, doesn't it Kel?"

"Yeah right, once you're under the spell of an enchantress and they know it, no going back!" laughed Kel. The telephone began to ring and Kel got up and went into the hallway to answer it, saving Laurie and myself from the possibility of further interrogation. Kel emerged a few seconds later and beckoned to Laurie.

"Who is it?" asked Laurie following Kel into the hallway.

"It's Jane for you," I heard him say.

Kel reappeared in the kitchen and sat down at the table with us.

"More wine anyone?" he asked holding the bottle poised. Ned held his glass up to be filled as I listened to Laurie's muffled voice out in the hallway, straining to make out his words. For the first time I am ashamed to say that I felt a pang of jealousy, something which took me by surprise. This was something else that I had been keeping from myself. I had always maintained that Jane was good to have in the background, so that Laurie would not want to take our astral relationship any further. However, with my feelings for Laurie becoming stronger, it was easier for me that she'd broken off the relationship. I probably wouldn't have realised these feelings if Laurie and Jane hadn't split up. Finally Laurie came back into the kitchen looking a little subdued and stunned, just as I had feared.

"Everything alright?" enquired Kel.

"She wants us to try again."

"And do you?"

"I don't know anymore. It's all very complicated, having a break from the relationship has made me view it from the outside. She wants to meet me tonight; maybe I'll feel differently when I see her again?"

"Someone sounds confused," put in Ned.

"Yes, that sums it all up nicely." Laurie gulped down the last of his wine.

I heard the front door creak open and Katri poked her head into the kitchen. "Hello, I thought I'd find you all in here." Velvet followed her, accompanied by Dylan and his four year old playmate, who was freckled and blue eyed.

"Hi everyone," beamed Velvet ushering the two boys into the kitchen.

"Do you want some soup?" enquired Kelsey.

"No thanks, we've already had our lunch. Velvet and I took the boys to a café in Amersham. Dylan's brought Joshua home to play. Dyl', why don't you take Josh in the garden? Daddy should have put the trampoline out for you while we were out." Dylan nodded, grinning at his friend, as Kel fetched them drinks of fruit juice.

"As it's such a beautiful day, why don't we all have our meeting on the lawn? Under the apple tree and we can keep an eye on the boys there too. I'll bring a couple of blankets out to sit on," said Kel.

The afternoon passed very pleasantly with the Faerie Ring. We planned our Summer Solstice ritual very quickly and then we lolled lazily in the sun while the Wharton's cat, Bella, sat in a heap of cat, purring like a well oiled engine among our sprawled bodies. Even Dylan and Joshua ran out of steam and started looking at comics on the lawn. At five o'clock I began to stir and announced that I would be leaving shortly.

"I'd better shoot off too; I've got an essay to get down to. Can I give you and Velvet a lift home Jessa?" asked Ned, drowsily rubbing his eyes.

"Thanks that would be good." I answered and Velvet nodded in agreement.

On the way home, as I had anticipated Ned started to push the conversation his way, probing for answers.

"Is Michael home then?"

"Not yet, he's working today at short notice, he'll be home early evening I expect."

"He seems to work a lot."

"He's good at his job, very involved in it. At the same time though it gives me the freedom I need to pursue my magical life."

"You like your freedom then?"

"Most of the time it suits me."

"So what's this with you and Laurie then?"

"I think I missed all this, Katri told me a bit about it at the café. Something about losing Laurie in Faerie Land?" enquired Velvet from the back seat of the car.

"Well yes and that was all there was to it. It's just like Kel explained, we click on a psychic level. What is this Ned, some sort of interrogation?" He grinned as we pulled up outside my house. He leant over and kissed me in a friendly way on the cheek and he blew a kiss to Velvet in the back of the car.

After Ned had dropped us off, Velvet came inside for an hour and we chatted over mugs of Earl Grey tea. We had another apprentice session and then I filled her in about the events of the night before. She had sat and listened on my sofa, enthralled.

"Do you know Velvet; I don't think that you ever told me about your experience with the King and Queen of Faerie, you know the one where you saw the apple tree door before anyone else?" Velvet smiled and curled her legs under herself on the sofa, as if she was a long-legged fawn.

"Is it worth a chocolate fudge crunch biscuit?" she said eyeing the plate of biscuits of the coffee table.

"It is worth the whole plate if you wish," I passed her the plate.

"Before I saw the door in the apple tree trunk I saw a green light surround the tree. It was like a green mist, the colour of ripe apples that sparkled like glittery faerie dust. I couldn't take my eyes off it and it was as if it was drawing me and my whole world in, everything else around the tree disappeared. Then the mist faded a little and the little doorway had become visible, I knew that was where I was going. I just had the feeling that everyone else could see it too, not just me. So as Katri told you, I blurted to everyone about the door, but it was really difficult and I almost had to force myself to come from a trance-like state to do it. Then once I had told everyone about the doorway, it was as if there was nothing holding me back, saying those words were like my key to enter. Then the garden totally blurred and disappeared and I wasn't aware of any of the other Ring members." She paused for a chocolate fudge crunch biscuit.

"Did you hear Laurie say *Jessamyn's Remembering place*?"

"No, not at all, although I instantly twigged that it was because there was the King and Queen of Faerie in the apple orchard, just like your experience. The King and Queen held out their hands and I knew that I must place my hands in theirs, as if I was handing myself over to them. I just felt that I had to trust them and that giving them my hands was to surrender myself. I knew that this was an act of faith because I didn't know where they were going to take me and I did have a feeling that they were taking me somewhere. What happened next was kind of weird." She gulped her tea and held yet another biscuit over the mug.

"May I dunk, do you mind?"

"Dunk away."

"Next thing, I fell asleep. It was weird because the moment I put my hands into theirs I fell unconscious."

"It's as if you were under their spell."

"That's what it felt like. I remember nothing from then on except that I had beautiful dreams and I was blissfully happy. I felt safe and enveloped in love, I just don't remember the details of the dream, just that I dreamt." She paused as if reliving the dreams in her mind.

"Then…?"

"Then I awoke still holding the hands of the Faerie King and Queen and a strange thing happened. The Faerie King said to me, *now you can go home and finish that essay you've been working on.* I didn't know what on earth he was talking about because although, I was working on an essay, I certainly didn't remember telling the Faerie King about it, I mean why on earth would I tell them about something as trivial as an essay? It's not exactly a spiritual revelation is it?"

"What was your essay about?"

"Shakespeare's *As You Like It* and the sense that people can appear something they are not, that a world can be created in which we believe, but it is an illusion. Ned will tell you that I had been struggling with it at the time. I said '*What?*' to the Faerie King, which I know doesn't sound a polite way to address a king and I felt a bit ashamed. But the Faerie King very patiently repeated his statement about going home to finish my essay and then I just stared at him completely dumbfounded and he must have thought me so stupid. I couldn't say anything because the penny had just dropped."

"I'm intrigued."

"Well of course it was much more to do with a message than the actual essay. You see the moment I had said '*What?*' I instantly remembered telling him about my essay before I had taken their hands. He had been trying to make me feel at ease once I had found myself in the apple orchard because I had been nervous. It was all very surreal, chatting to the King and Queen of Faerie about an unfinished essay!"

"This is another *Remembering* isn't it?"

"I knew you would recognize it Jessa. Ned still thinks there is some spiritual significance in my handing in an essay late!" We both laughed.

"The meaning of course was that we come from the spiritual realms of faerie, but we do not always remember it in this life, unless we are given an intense and personal reminder from the Land of Faerie itself. The sleep and dreaming were symbolic of life and that we go through it unaware of our spiritual state. My jolt of remembering from the Faerie King was my awakening, just like yours. It was him saying to me, *"Remember this life is all but a dream, but until you know that it is a dream you cannot awaken from it. From then on you can experience*

135

life in awareness, knowing that this life is only a dream from which you can consciously manipulate the events."

"We must consciously live the dream."

"Yes, and remember *the Remembering.*

* * *

When Velvet had gone, I spent the rest of the evening writing up an entry into my Book of Elfin. I still hadn't written up the Coombe Hill ritual from some time ago. I wanted to keep busy and take my mind off the fact that Laurie was spending the evening with Jane. However, I think I should have chosen a task that involved less thinking about Laurie, as writing about the ritual and Laurie's part in it, invoked my thoughts and feelings for him even more strongly. At around nine, I heard Michael's car pull up. I instinctively snapped my Book of Elfin shut and stuffed it under the settee. I heard Michael slam the front door shut and shout from the hallway.

"What a day!" He stormed into the living room where I had picked up my sewing and was threading a button on a jacket. "Jessa, we have to talk," he demanded. He obviously meant business and I placed my sewing down beside me at once.

"Why the sudden urgency?"

"Because I've had time to have a good think and I've been far too reasonable. You've been keeping something from me for years and now you expect me just to accept it."

"It took a lot of courage for me to tell you."

"Why couldn't you have done it a bit earlier into the relationship, like when we first met for instance?"

"What difference would it have made? You don't like it now, so you wouldn't have liked it then."

"Maybe we wouldn't have got this far if I'd known about it then."

"You wouldn't have married me?"

"You got it."

"You really hate it that much?"

"You don't live in the real world Jessa, you never have done and now I know why, it all fits into place."

"I do live in the real world; it's just that my real is different to yours."

"I've got to be honest and say that all this stuff about magic and faeries existing in the twenty-first century is all fantasy to me and it doesn't feel right. It feels alien in my life."

"I'm not asking you to live in my world, just to accept what has been going on right under your nose all our married life."

"But you've been deceiving me Jessa. You've been lying all this time and leading a double life with friends I've never even met. Even now I know about it, you've insisted that there are secrets that you can't tell me." He grabbed hold of my shoulders, startling me and looking straight into my eyes, staring a hard, questioning stare. "I have never been a part of you and even now, even though I know this secret of yours, you still won't let me in. You have to ask yourself whether you really want to be with me or not. We are both living half a life with one another, me with my work demands and you with your odd faerie ways, which I shall never understand."

"I know that, I've been struggling against this life of ours for years."

"I'm not sure that I want to struggle any longer."

"What are you saying Michael, are you leaving me?"

"I'm going to stay with my brother in London for a couple of weeks."

"And after that?"

"I'll probably come home and we can talk it over more rationally: when I'm less angry would be better. I don't want to throw four years of marriage away in the heat of the moment." He paused for a second. "Would there be any chance of you giving up your faeriecraft or whatever you call it?"

"No Michael, none at all, it's who I am. You can never stop being a Faerie Priestess."

"Not even to save our marriage?"

"Then what would you have left, Michael? An empty shell of a person, who lives for her husband, who is not around ninety percent of the time anyway? I wonder if you would work fewer hours for me?"

"But it's my job, that's different."

"Yes, but you don't need to work the hours you do. You are driven by it, Michael. Being a Priestess is my vocation in life. A Priestess has a calling the same way that a nun does, only it is a magical one, the Faerie Queen calls her, but I don't expect you will understand that."

"You can't really liken this new-age crap to a nun surely? You cannot expect me to take that seriously. You're living in cloud-cuckoo land and unless you snap out of it there isn't any future for us." He looked down at the carpet as if those were his final words on the matter.

"It's not new-age crap. The Faerie religion has been around for thousands of years. Can't you take life a little less seriously, Michael and see that it makes me happy, it fulfils me and I'm not hurting anyone by being this way?" There was a long aching silence as dusk fell outside and the birds sang their summer evening songs. Finally, he lifted up his head sadly and placed his warm hand over mine. .

"I had such high hopes for this marriage, such hopes. My parents will be heartbroken, they think the world of you, as you know," he said quietly.

"It's not over yet Michael, it doesn't have to be over, and we might be able to work through this." I said squeezing his hand, feeling miserably guilty.

"I'll sleep in the spare room tonight and I'll go to Steven's house tomorrow morning." He got up to go upstairs and when he left the room I felt nothing. I felt only numbness and strangely as if I was a character in a play, acting out a role. I was the wicked temptress, the woman that had cheated on her husband. I was the character that the audience allowed themselves to despise, for no one likes an unfaithful woman.

I felt deeply sorry for Michael, but at the same time the breath of inevitability seemed to pervade the room. In my play I seemed to know the next scene, even though my part was unrehearsed. However, even though I had woken up to reality and realized it was a play that I was in, I couldn't stop the fact that life was a play and would still go on around me. The numbness filled me as if it really was a feeling and I knew that I would not be able to sleep. For a woman who had had a relationship with two men that morning, I suddenly had none at all, for even Laurie was with Jane trying to patch things up. I suddenly felt relief and a gap in the feelings, both sexual and emotional for these two men: a place where I may rest from the surging passions that had flowed through me so violently over the past few weeks.

I crept upstairs silently, as if I was some kind of apparition and quietly collected my felt handbag from our bedroom. I left a short note to Michael, just to say where I was and then I left the house, clicking the front door behind me as if I had been an intruder, not wanting to disturb the occupants.

I took the short walk to the Wharton's house as if I was in some kind of soporific trance. As I approached I saw that the kitchen light was on. It looked cosy within their house and as I had stood at the front door I hesitated to knock as it seemed a shame to invade the magic spell of the outside view, by entering into the house itself and becoming a part of it.

"Jessamyn!" Katri exclaimed in surprise as she stood at the open front door. Katri didn't need much of an explanation; she seemed to have a feeling that my marriage was not a contented one. As a fellow Priestess, it went without saying that she would support me in any crisis at a moments notice. A Faerie Ring is like a faerie seeker's support group/refuge/social and spiritual group all rolled into one. I knew that Laurie was out for the evening with Jane, otherwise I wouldn't have gone there. Kelsey was working upstairs in his office.

Katri had made me a cup of tea and sat down beside me on the sofa, brushing her black hair from her eyes. "I've never met Michael, but he doesn't know you does he?"

"No, that is how the trouble began. I started to let him into the real me and he's fled. I know that I must be difficult to live with because of my secretive ways. When it comes to the otherworldly experiences that I have, I cannot begin to get him to understand. I'm just an over imaginative woman in his eyes."

"Well Laurie seems to be having the same kind of problem with Jane," said Katri dunking a digestive biscuit into her tea. "Do you want one?" she asked, offering me the biscuit tin and I shook my head in response. "And he's probably getting back together with her as we speak." I could not offer a reply, as I dare not imagine Laurie and Jane together, not now I had become so entwined with feelings for him.

"She doesn't understand that he's a magical person. She's an earthy practical sort of person and they're total opposites really, she's an accountant and he's an archaeologist, God knows how they met. But sometimes a spiritual person needs an earthy partner to anchor them; otherwise they just float through life with no purpose. But truly when it comes down to it a Faerie Priest needs to marry a Faerie Priestess or at least someone of a similar spiritual persuasion, otherwise there's discord."

"Is that your philosophy on faeriecraft relationships?"

"Yes it is, and I'm sticking to it," she giggled. "There's more trouble if you're in a Faerie Ring because the other partner becomes jealous with the close relationship the spouse has with her fellow seekers."

"So I'm doomed then?" I laughed.

"Yes, quite, quite doomed Jessa, there's no hope at all." We both laughed. "You've got to marry your Faerie Priest, your magical partner and all your problems will be solved. So Laurie it is then, he is your true magical partner, for you are the Queen of Cobwebs and he the King. That's it settled then, I've solved all your problems, see how good I am, you should have come to have tea and biscuits with me ages ago." I smiled weakly and suddenly felt sick, I wanted to tell Katri everything right from the beginning, but I simply sipped my tea.

"I'll make up the spare bed for you, it's quite comfy, Laurie can vouch for that."

"What about Laurie, won't he be back soon? I hadn't planned to stay over."

"Laurie is going straight on to his parent's house for tonight as they live very near where he and Jane have gone, from what I can gather." With that she disappeared to fetch some bedding.

I did not sleep peacefully at all that night, for I dreamt that a strange faerie creature wearing a ragged dress was knotting my hair. As she went about her mischievous work while sitting on the edge of my pillow, all I can remember is her chanting the words, ' tangle, tangle, tangle'. She seemed to take great pleasure in her knotting and I decided that I did not like her at all.

I was awoken by Dylan, mistaking me for Laurie. I had opened my eyes to see him in his *Star Wars* pyjamas, sucking his thumb and twiddling his hair.

"Is Mummy out of bed yet?" I enquired; glad to be awake and away from the clutches of the knotty faerie.

"No she doesn't get up until *Scooby Doo* is on," he answered.

"Is that on soon?"

"No, not for ages."

"Oh. Do you want some breakfast Dylan?"

"Can I have 'Coco Pops'?"

"Is that what you usually have then?"

"No, they're for treats. Can I?"

"All right."

Dylan and I sat before *Lazy Town* and ate 'Coco Pops' together on the floor. He laughed at the pranks while I sat transfixed at the marvellous physique of Sporticus the hero. The words, '*tangle, tangle, tangle*', kept forcing their way into my thoughts, as if they were unwanted intruders, just like their speaker had been, the knotty faerie. It was evident that my life was a tangle and I had tied myself up in a knot. I knew that I had to go back to my house. I had left because reminders of my marriage were of course seeped into the walls and every single thing there. I had thought that being away from the house would perhaps have given me a clearer head. Now, however, I felt an impulse to return and I did not know why. I dressed and not wanting to wake Katri and Kelsey, I wrote them a note explaining my absence, and left it on the kettle. I kissed Dylan on the forehead. "Bye, Auntie Jessa," he mumbled.

On my way home I passed the entrance to the wood where my Faerie Ring usually worked. It had been a beautiful sunny morning and I stopped to notice cobwebs glistening as they swung in the light breeze, bedewed and suspended within an abundant patch of stinging nettles. It seemed as if the woods were inviting me to enter, as had happened before on a few occasions. It was still quite early in the morning and there was no one around that I could see. I could not resist the beckoning of the spider's web spiral, my favourite portal to the Land of Faerie.

Impulsively I began to enter the woods and I soon took the usual route off the public footpath. I followed the ivy covered track, heading towards the Magic Place. As I caught sight of the circle of trees, I gasped to myself at the mossy altar which sparkled like a cloth of green velvet, sprinkled with diamonds. The sunlight had caught the dewy moss at a moment of magic and as the speckly shafts of early light fell upon the copse, I entered its silent chapel with reverence. I knelt before the altar, suddenly aware that I had no gift to leave for the fey people. Feeling that I must leave at least something of beauty for Queen Mab, I undid the middle buttons on my blouse and in the centre of my bra was sewn a beautiful embroidered red rose. I tugged at the small red stitches which kept it in place and soon loosened it with my fingernails. I placed it on the altar and said a few words to Queen Mab.

In the unique silence of the early morning woodland, I felt a peacefulness. I knew that now was the time to start anew and untangle my knotted life. Symbolically I made a small knot in some of the strands of my long hair. "Knot of sadness breaks away, untangle this life, starting today." I kissed the knot and then broke it off from the rest of my hair with my fingers. I placed the knot of dark hair beside the red cotton rose on the moss altar.

"Knotty faerie of my dreams,
stitch my life at the seams.
As above so below,
by this knot make it so."

I giggled to myself at my badly concocted verse and felt relieved at the little spell I had enacted. As I got up and turned to leave down the ivy pathway, I noticed the knot of hair and the cotton rose both got blown away by the breeze. I knew then that the spell had reached the ether and had a chance of working for me.

Chapter Ten

Beguiling & Bewitching Place

'Here we begin the hidden knowing.
What once slept, rekindles to bring us
something we already know.
The secrets are hidden in the earth
and the fey are the keepers.
It may take an archaeologist to reveal the past
that will bring us knowledge
of the present...'

The Faerie Mound

As I turned the corner out of the public footpath, my house had come into view and there I saw something which instantly made me stop and stare. There in the driveway was parked Michael's silver Audi and all the curtains at the windows of the house were drawn as if he was still at home. I felt peculiar as I walked the last few metres to the front door, for this was not what I had anticipated. Feeling slightly nervous I had quietly slipped the front door key into the lock and entered to find the house as silent as a séance.

I crept upstairs for there was no life on the ground floor and as I had peeped around our bedroom door, my eyes fell upon a sleeping, fully clothed Michael. He was lying face down on the bed, as if in the deepest of slumbers. When I had opened the door wider, I gasped for the whole of the bedroom floor was covered with the contents of my magical trunk. Every item had been unpacked and examined, even my treasured Book of Elfin had been read and was left open at the page where I had written my last entry. There were incense jars and pots of herbs strewn across the floor, my crystal wand was now glinting in the rays of the morning sun, which filtered through a chink in the curtains. When I had first told Michael that I was a Faerie Priestess, I had mentioned to him that I would show him my magical trunk. However, events had got in the way and finally I had forgotten all about it, evidently Michael hadn't and now he had got to the point where he had helped himself. I wondered what had made him decide not to go to Steven's house last night and whether he still intended to go.

The telephone began to ring and I decided to answer it downstairs, so as not to wake Michael.

"It's me," said Laurie. "Is tomorrow night still on? It's hard for me to get away, but I think that I can make it if you want to go ahead with it."

"I need to do this Laurie, even if it's only to finish something with a complete ending. Let's not end this, with everything hanging in the air."

"I'll be there," he promised, and then hung up as if someone had caught him out.

I sat on the floor in the glow of Laurie's voice, for about twenty minutes. I felt drenched in Laurie unable to concentrate on anything else. He was obviously back together with Jane and I realised that my dreams of spending my life with him were unrealistic. We really could only experience one another in the spiritual, for there were too many complications in the real world to bring about a physical union between us. Besides, I suddenly realised that would make our relationship into the mundane, with all the messy problems that every other couple has to deal with on a daily basis. Even though I longed to feel the physical touch of his bare skin against mine, I knew that the touching of our astral bodies was a sensual and celestial ecstasy that few people had ever experienced and were ever likely to until their own death. I had to hang on to my real and physical relationship with Michael otherwise life with Laurie would mean never touching my feet on the ground again. As Katri had said the night before, that sometimes a spiritual person needed a practical person to anchor them, that was very true in my case.

I had started to make myself a cup of tea when Michael shocked me, as I had turned around to find him standing motionless behind me. "You're back, actually I didn't think that you were coming back at all," he said blankly, staring into my eyes. I could not tell if he was still angry with me or not.

"I just felt that I needed to be back at the house. I seemed to do all the sorting out in my mind that I needed to do; it was pointless to stay away any longer. When are you going to Steven's, I was surprised to find you here?"

"I've decided not to go." He sighed and sat down at the kitchen table. "It was Jenny that made me angry with you."

"Jenny?" I asked incredulously.

"I had to tell someone about your confession to me, I was just so confused and quite frankly when she knew that something was up, she wouldn't rest until she'd wheedled it out of me."

"Why did you have to confide in her of all people? She's been after you from the very first day you employed her. Of course she'd jump at the chance of making me look like the wicked wife and turn you against me. She knows all our business now I suppose and she has knowledge of something very real to hold against me if she chooses." I began to feel angry as my quiet and long held fears about Jenny were being realised. He reached in his trouser pocket and pulled out a small ornate silver key that I recognised immediately. "I found this in your jewellery box, I admit I was going through your things to find it. I confess that I've looked at everything in your trunk. I'm sorry if I've taken a liberty, but you were going to show it to me one day." He slowly and deliberately handed me back the key to my magical trunk.

"Have you satisfied your curiosity?"

"Quite. I have read the book that you call your Book of Elfin from cover to cover and although I still cannot say that I understand why you do it, I'm beginning to get a feel for what it's all about. I also understand why you have kept it secret for so long, I wouldn't have believed you if you'd have told me all the experiences you've had in your faerie rituals. You really do live in another world Jessa and its very different to mine. I thought we had a lot in common when we met with our careers in books, but we also have a lot that separates us." He paused and gently took my hand and I sat down beside him aching for him not to leave me, knowing that he had something important to say and hoping that it would be what I wanted to hear.

"I spent a very long time last night studying your life and I compared it with my own. I know that since we've been married our time together has been snatched weekends when I haven't been working and lots of long distance phone calls. You're not all to blame for the mess we've found ourselves in. We've got to change everything if we want to make it work, you and your secrets and me and my work. I know that I work excessively and I don't really need to put in so many hours."

"When I go into the office tomorrow I'll have a word with Alex about my schedule. There are others who could easily share my work load, but the truth is, I like to have all the control. I could cut my hours in a small way without losing too much status in the company"

"Are you sure you can see yourself doing that? Your work is your life, Michael."

"And you should be. I don't want to end up a workaholic divorcee now do I?" He had squeezed my hand and kissed it. "There's a performance of '*A Midsummer Night's Dream*' on at Regents Park tonight, would you like me to ring for tickets?"

"We haven't been to the theatre since our first wedding anniversary. I would love that."

"Then that's what we'll do."

From that moment I felt as if I could see the pathway of our marriage stretching before us and we were walking along it together. I felt that years of secrecy, of keeping faeriecraft from him and the strain of being alone a lot of the time were slipping away from me. I had real hopes that this was a new start for us. I hoped that I could sort my head out too and make him happy, because I knew he was trying very hard to make things work.

We spent a beautiful evening together witnessing the magic of '*A Midsummer Night's Dream*'. The faerie characters were spellbinding to me and Oberon and Titania caught my imagination as they have never failed to do. As I sat watching the play in the crowded theatre stalls, I had to keep reminding myself that I was really there with Michael, watching my favourite play, when only last night I had thought that I may be facing a life without him.

Once at home we drank white wine together in bed amid the room that was imbrued in darkness except for a streak of moonlight which stained the carpet and part of our bed in its silvered light. Then we made love under the Lady Moon's luminescence and he fulfilled the senses of the earthy, feeling self. I wanted him and only him in the moments when we clung to one another, knowing that this was the right place for both of us to be. It was as if he had been away from me for a very long time and I felt as I had when we made love for the very first time. For when we were new to one another I had not been closed to him and I had wanted to share my secret life with him. However, after a while it had become apparent that I could not divulge my secrets and by then it was too late, I had fallen deeply in love with him. I am glad now that I did not have a real life physical affair with Laurie, but he still beckons and I can never deny my astral, spiritual self its expression, for that is one part of me that Michael can never touch.

After Michael had drifted asleep and I lay alone in the gentle moonlight, I felt peace within myself. It was one of the most pleasant sensations I had had for many months. I felt that I had worked through a lot of feelings and all the impassioned events of the past couple of weeks had culminated in releasing a part of me that I did not realise needed fulfilling. My spiritual-self did not have to be in conflict with my earthly-self as I had thought. I suddenly recognised in the penetrating stillness of the night, that my nix and everyday self could co-exist. I could not deny one or the other, lest one should wither away and die. The dilemma had been resolved within me, for if Michael could live knowingly with a Priestess and Laurie could be met nixly, faeriewitchly on the astral plane, both lovers who fulfilled different parts of me would be satisfied.

As long as the astral relationship was never spoken of, it remained untouched and therefore potentially unreal. If I had left Michael I would have found some sort of spiritual identity with Laurie, however, I would have lost my mind as well as any sense of reality. If I had given Laurie up I would have lost my spiritual purpose altogether, leaving me in a prosaic prison. Both parts of me had to exist in harmony with one another, and as long as they both stayed in their own worlds I could still experience the sexual poetry of faeriecraft and also the passionate security of married life.

That night I dreamt of Laurie, but it was a dream of my own encapsulation. I did not leave my body, consciously anyway, and he did not call the fetch of me. I dreamt that we were at the Magic Place in the woods, but I was unaware of my surroundings, for the trees appeared like a blurred curtain of darkness. While he kissed my robed body I was as if a mannequin simply drinking in the experience and playing the part of a passive innocent. His kisses on my neck were like a pleasurable poison and although his kissing made my body ache with longing for him, I could not respond in any way to his needs. What made it worse, was that in the blurry dream atmosphere as each kiss came and went, the next one was more exquisite than the last and the skin on my neck felt as if it needed those shocking kisses. My skin became sensitive to the pleasures and even the slight touch of the curls of his hair on my face as he bent over me, felt like the scorch of one of his kisses.

"You look as if you've got a rash on your neck." I opened my eyes at the sound of Michael's voice as he stood at the side of the bed, doing his tie up. He smelt of soap and shampoo, as I got out of bed and stumbled into the bathroom. In the mirror my neck looked a little red and I wondered if it could have been scratches from Michael's unshaven kisses from our lovemaking the night before. My neck felt tingly and I felt aroused. The dream was still pervading my aura and I wasn't quite awake yet.

"Am I late Michael?"

"No, it's all right I'm early. I wanted to get into the office before everyone else so that I could have a word with Alex about my hours."

"Are you sure about this?" I asked coming out of the bathroom to face him. He nodded and smiling he kissed me lightly on the cheek.

"I'll see you later then. I'm playing squash after work, so I'll be late back. Don't wait up for me, but I'll ring you. Be careful when you're flying to work on that broomstick of yours." I swiped him playfully as he went out of the door, feeling a warm sensation inside of me that perhaps things may turn out well for us after all.

The bedroom floor was strewn with the contents of my magical trunk, as I had not had time to clear it all up. I only hoped that my mother did not pay me a surprise visit while my whole occult life was displayed for all to see. I would have to clear it up after work. The shrill sound of Michael's mobile phone ringing broke the silence and I suddenly saw it light up momentarily among my Faerie Priestess paraphernalia. I grabbed it while it was still ringing and ran downstairs calling after him, but I was too late. As I opened the front door I saw his silver Audi already driving away at the end of our road. I sighed and closed the door, knowing that he would be lost that day without his mobile. I pressed the button to answer the call in case it was something urgent and found that it was a text message. As I read the text I had to sit down on the floor in the hallway, as I felt so upset I could not stand.

'Looking forward to tonight honey,
did she buy the squash excuse?

Luv and kisses – Jenny

xxxxxxxxxxxxxxxxxxxxxx '.

I felt as if my insides had been manually removed without anaesthesia and all my resolve had gone. I had been fretting all this time about hurting Michael's feelings when it looked like he hadn't a care for me. My mind spun back to the book fair and how Jenny had been all over him then. I'd had my suspicions about her from that day, but had automatically cancelled it out as I had always thought that Michael would never do that to me. My fingers accessed the previous messages on Michael's phone, even though I did not want to find them, it seemed my fingers did. Sure enough there were similar and some sexually explicit texts from Jenny. It made what I had been up to with Laurie, look like two twelve year olds holding hands in the park. My stomach physically lurched at some of the messages and there was no doubt at all, this was a full blown grown-up affair, whips and all. I suddenly felt quite justified at my union with Laurie. From the dates on some of the messages, this affair had been going on for some months before Laurie and I had got together. I couldn't quite believe that I had been blind to it all these months. I felt nauseous at the thought of Michael and Jenny together, and I couldn't even see what he saw in her, apart from the fact that she was available. I wondered now if my marriage to Michael could be saved. It was certainly all a pretence for Michael, feigning a reconciliation with me, perhaps just for a quiet life.

What to do now? I pondered. I put the mobile phone in my pocket and decided to act ignorant of its whereabouts if he asked, while I came up with a decent plan. At least I had one consolation, I would be seeing Laurie tonight and we would be alone, maybe for the last time, but I had that to look forward to for one whole treasured day.

The day scraped past at the library and I felt sad within myself. Why couldn't I enjoy real life like Rose and Sheila at the library? Their feet were firmly on the ground. They knew of no other place in their imagination than the Mills and Boon novels that they read in their morning tea breaks. That was as far as their imaginations ventured, and it was a safe distance, unlike myself, who had fallen into a nix inhabited well and didn't want to get out.

My mind was in one place all day and that was with Laurie in the woods. At least I did not have any lying to do where Michael was concerned, as he would be out all evening in another's arms and maybe even her handcuffs if Jenny's messages were anything to go by. As my day at the library was winding down, my mind fell unwillingly upon the matter of Michael's mobile phone. I did not feel that I wanted to confront him with the issue yet. *If he could be sly, then so could I,* I thought. I scrounged a used padded envelope from the office and stuck an address label on the outside. I then addressed it to Michael at his publisher's address in London. I placed the mobile phone inside and with it a handwritten note, I wrote simply:

Don't forget to check your messages.

Jessa.

I then placed the envelope, along with some heavy thoughts of how he would react, in the library post tray. I knew that it would catch the evening post and it would be on his desk for the following morning. Job done.

It was a hauntingly dusky summer evening as I crossed the road to the mouth of the footpath, where I was to meet up with Laurie. This was the time of day when the veil is thin between the worlds. I watched circles of gnats fly above the little river and a bat flew silently over my head. Dusk was the time when the day creatures overlapped with the night creatures and things were difficult to perceive in the half-light. The in-between time that belongs to faerie.

I was nervous as I waited for him in my long blue summer dress and I had my down-to-the-ground lilac velvet dress in a bag under my arm. I had looked at my watch, it said ten past nine, he was late and I thought that perhaps he wasn't going to turn up. *Perhaps he was with Jane and he could not get away.*

She would not understand the relationship between a Faerie Priest and Priestess of the art. I did not think that she could comprehend that we only existed for one another in the spiritual realms. She would not understand that a man and a woman could be quite, quite alone in the woods and never once touch one another, except to kiss on the cheek, nothing more in the physical way. If she knew of us, she would not understand or trust that we had never shared one another's bodies, and were ever likely to. People who are not of the magical arts would assume that we were going to make love to one another in the woods, as soon as our spouse's backs were turned. I knew that Laurie and I would barely touch tonight, but that we would share all the sexual joy that two people could. This Jane would never understand and if she ever knew that Laurie had a Priestess, I think that it would be the end of his magical career.

I heard faint, quick footsteps coming along the riverside gravel pathway. I could see a hazy figure coming towards me.

"Jessa is that you?"

"Yes, it's me."

"I'm late, I'm sorry." He kissed me quickly on the cheek.

"Everything made me behind, work was very involved today. I don't know how I got away and then Jane rang while I was at the Wharton's place. I'm moving back in with her tomorrow, it's what I want, for the time being anyway. She's all I've ever known, until… well, it feels right." He did not seem to be able to look at me when he spoke.

"You don't have to apologise for getting your life sorted out. I don't think that you and I would ever have worked out in reality. We need someone to keep us earthed, we can't live fantasies, we can't always be with phantom lovers, life just wouldn't function anymore. You need your Jane and I need my Michael, but at the same time you have to come home sometimes to your Faerie Priestess and me to my Priest." He smiled and kissed me again on the forehead. I did not want to tell him about the affair between Michael and Jenny, in fact I didn't think that I could tell anybody. I didn't want to make him feel guilty that he should be with me and not Jane, now that he had made his decision.

"Someone's been doing a lot of thinking." We started to walk along the pathway which led to the woods and the Magic Place where we were going to work. The light was fading quickly and our footsteps echoed in the clear night air. "Are you nervous?"

"Why are you?"

"I don't know why I am, but I've got butterflies with boots on storming around my stomach," he said smiling.

"I'm nervous, I have been all day. We've never held a Faerie Circle alone together."

"Then it's about time we did."

As we reached the Magic Place, it had become very dark and the summer air felt heavy with the woody scent of the trees. Just as we neared the circle of trees, Laurie gasped and then, I saw for myself what was making him stop still and breathless. On the tree trunk altar sat a faerie woman appearing completely to be made from glittering moonlight. She was the most bewitchingly beautiful creature I had ever seen and she took my breath away. All I could see was her; nothing else existed in those moments. She smiled at us, a secret smile; she seemed to be aware of our presence. On her silvery moonlit hair she wore a crown of white daisies and her long flowing, down-to-her-toes dress was stitched with real white poppies, she seemed to belong in a meadow. She looked familiar as she beckoned us to come closer. Laurie seemed rooted to the spot, but I knew that I must take her hand, that she was here for us, that she had waited for us to arrive that night.

I walked slowly forward, her presence making me feel slightly dizzy and as if I was taking part in a dream that I was conscious of. She filled my every senses and made me feel as if I was full of stars, full of the swirling universe in my very self. She reached out her hand of light and blinked her enormous elfin eyes and then I knew, I knew who she was. "Queen Mab," I whispered and she smiled her entrancing smile and burst before our eyes into a thousand beams of moonlight, scattering around the circle of trees, filling our woodland circle with her presence. I took her place on the tree trunk altar and Laurie knelt before me, placing his outstretched arms on the tops of my thighs. We breathed in the night air deeply together, both too in awe at what we had experienced to speak or move.

I took a deep breath and stood before Laurie, taking off my shoes and dropping them to the leafy floor. I changed my dress and Laurie also put on his brown velvet robe. Queen Mab had left in her wake an electrifyingly sexual atmosphere. I was experiencing a heightened sense of awareness, as if everything was more real and magical than usual. I felt the fecundity of nature, of the woodland become a part of me and I was one with the whispering trees and the sparkling black night air. Laurie began the Faerie Fivefold Kiss in silence, the honouring of a Priestess and the atmosphere was charged. And as in my dream, his kisses scorched me with their intent, when he reached the final kiss he whispered, "Blessed Be your lips, which speak of the secret elfin ways."

We then stood opposite one another, and after we had cast our Faerie Circle we needed no candles, the moonlight showed us the way. We needed no incense, as the woodland air was heady. Every second seemed like a minute, every minute seemed like an hour, time had been suspended for us and we belonged in Queen Mab's time. It was the time that existed in the place between the worlds, where every moment sparkled with aliveness. Laurie knelt slowly before me and I entered into a deep meditative state and together we saw and felt the moon-drenched Faerie Queen above us.

Laurie directed the moon's energy upwards through my chakras; I felt in an exhilarating altered state. Each breath he took was my breath; every image he visualised of the Faerie Queen of Moonlight was also my visualisation. Finally directing the energy to my crown chakra, he visualised the image of the exquisite Faerie Queen, so that her shimmering figure of beauty covered my own body and he saw the Queen of all Faerie standing before him. Laurie then delivered his *charge* and as he did so it became the most profound stage of drawing down the moon. I entered a deep state of consciousness and became one with the words and the images. Laurie's words danced brightly in my mind as he said the invocation:

"Faerie Queen, secret and divine,
the enchanted orb draws me to your lights.
I wish to share the moon's delights,
Catching moonbeams to be mine.

In between time and space,
Beguiling and bewitching place,
Moon shafts descend to me,
In this faerie circle be.

Faerie Queen, take my hand,
Transport me to Faerie Land,
Where moonbeams land just like snow.
This silvery light I wish to know."

As soon as Laurie had delivered these words I saw the moonlit Faerie Queen descend within me and I felt profoundly alive, complete and magical; in possession of my own power. It was the most spiritual and fulfilling experience, I felt the constellations move within me, as if I was a mirror of the night's starry sky. I could see the moonlight sparkling and shimmering throughout my body and aura. I felt bound closer to Laurie than I had ever felt before. At that time, in those complete and magical moments with Laurie as my Faerie Priest, I knew that this was what I had been put on earth to do. This was my place of power, this was where I was to find the real me, peace lying waiting for me to unshroud it. This was where my strength was, in this place of power I had finally found the key.

Chapter Eleven

Truly Nixly, Faeriewitchly

'Love is not love
Which alters when it alteration finds,
Or bends with the remover to remove:-

O no! It is an ever-fixed mark
That looks on tempests, and is never shaken;
It is the star to every wandering bark…'

William Shakespeare, True Love

As I sat at my desk that morning in the library, looking out of the window at the drizzly weather, I felt a blissful sense of contentment. Last night's *drawing down the moon* in all its ecstasy had left me with a feeling of attainment and clarity, as if the last few weeks had culminated in one final spiritual union between me, the Nixie, and my archaeologist. Although it was unspoken I now knew what all this had been about and, most importantly, I sensed strongly what the way forward would be for us. We had both been through turmoil to be together, but it did not have to be like that, for neither of us was hurting anyone by being entwined and, in fact, who would believe us anyway if they knew? What was important was that life was experienced to its fullest possible capacity; that in the end there are no right and wrongs to life, just experiences. Sometimes it is good to do things to extremes.

I had only seen Michael in bed last night and he had gone to work by the time I had got up. We had not had a conversation beyond one syllable, due to the fact that I had been almost asleep when he had finally arrived home from '*squash*'. I pictured him in his office at work and I knew that he must have received my package by now. I felt apprehensive at the thought and wondered what would happen that night when he came home.

Besides, these thoughts, I was basking in the bliss of the night before, everyone in the library seemed different today. People appeared more beautiful, the drizzly rain outside felt like magic falling on the pavement rather than the disappointment that rain usually brings. Time felt expansive and full of possibilities and I felt that nothing could ever be ordinary again. I knew that I had reached some kind of inner completion; I had reached the point in my life where many of my past struggles had been resolved. I did not have to do anything more to achieve this, but experience an intensity that had now metamorphosed into a feeling of being at peace with myself and with the universe. I felt in a position to attain my aspirations in life and even Michael's affair appeared to be a mere blip. This was my zenith, my time of power and fulfilment. I felt that I was in harmony with myself for the first time since I had been a child. I had only glimpsed this harmony while making love, while meditating in the Ring, whilst experiencing another's art, but it had only ever been for a moment. Now it was mine to keep, for I had earned it and I deserved it.

Rose broke my cogitating spell all of a sudden and called me over to the photocopier to ask me something about copyright.

"Perhaps you would be kind enough to look it up for me Jessamyn and put it on my desk when you've got a moment. I see you've got a few moments to spare. While we're on the subject of..." Her voice trailed away and she stared over my shoulder in the direction of my desk. I knew I had been about to receive a reprimand so I did not prompt her to finish her sentence, but merely revelled in the rare Rose silence. After a few moments with a look of complete disbelief on her face, she threw her hands in the air and just walked away from me, I caught part of her scorning.

"It's one rule for Jessamyn and another for everyone else. What's the point...?" With that she left the reference library, and left me in peace.

I had no idea what had ruffled her feathers so violently until, baffled I sat down at my desk again to continue my work. On my computer screen was sticky taped a large silver envelope, with my name written on the front. I knew the handwriting immediately, for it was Laurie's. Rose must have seen Laurie stick it there for my many friends, who visit the library while I am meant to be working – are a particular loathing of hers. I smiled to myself and pulled the envelope off the screen. There had been no sign of Laurie but his cheek had made Rose livid. As I had opened the silver envelope the red handkerchief he had been wearing dropped onto my desk, it was still tied in a knot. I gasped, quickly putting it in my jacket pocket, hoping that no one had seen. Although no one who saw it would have thought anything of it, it had personal significance, deeply private meaning. Also in the envelope was a note, it read:

Dearest Jessamyn,

Returned – one physical reminder.
I need no reminding, for my nixie priestess and I are bound together astrally, for time without end. Keep it, burn it, do what you will with it.
I know that you will want to know this, last night while 'drawing down the moon' I saw your hair and face in moonlight, but the moonlight appeared to me as water. I believe I saw you as the Nix. I have never seen a sight so utterly possessing.

Love,

Laurie xxx

I folded up the note neatly and put it in the same pocket as the handkerchief. Suddenly conscious of the readers around me, I decided to visit the toilets to re-read it on my own. I had closed the door behind me in a cubicle and leant my back against the door, reading the letter over and over again and the word nix kept leaping out of the page at me. Ever since Laurie had come into my life, so had the Nix faerie, appearing to Laurie, Michael and myself in many different ways. By now she felt a part of me, as I wore the Nix-like personality within me. What had happened when Laurie and I had started to meet on the astral plane was that we had begun to explore our deeper, untouched selves and in my case, the self I was afraid of. All through this the Nix had been a mysterious, entrancing creature, who had appeared when I least expected it. This was the summer that the Nixie had bewitched me and in turn I had bewitched Laurie, for a Priestess, however good she intends to be, cannot help being ever so slightly wicked.

The Nix had chosen me to show me myself. The side of myself that I had dare not uncover, was the so-called 'dark side' or my real adventurous side. Now instead of being afraid of her, I knew that I had to accept her and then she would stop haunting me. These thoughts empowered me, for the first time in years. I felt at one with myself and in control, in possession of my deepest feelings. All of a sudden I knew what I had to do. I needed to banish my nix: to thank her for the magic and the unveiling of my secret-self and ask her to leave me in peace. I had no more need of her in my life. Next week was the Summer Solstice and the Faerie Ring would be meeting: it was the best opportunity I had to send her on her way and for me to assert my freedom.

After work I had hurried home through the light summer scented rain to make sure that I would arrive before Michael. Still in my coat I went to the bedroom and collected the stars that Laurie had given me from my underwear drawer. I put them, the red love knot and Laurie's letter in a small velvet bag that I kept in my magical trunk. I then went to the garden and rummaged around in our untidy shed, until I found a hand trowel. I chose my spot carefully; somewhere that Michael, or anyone else for that matter, would never be likely to dig. It was in the little herb patch that Michael considered my bit of the garden. I then dug as deep a hole as I could manage, constantly listening out for Michael's homecoming. I did not want to have to do any explaining, not now that I was burying my unsaid life. Now was the beginning of the end of an episode in my life that I always wanted to remain untouched.

I kissed the velvet bag containing the objects and then dropped it into the earthy hole. As I began to pile the earth back into the hole I whispered a rhyme which I had made up in my lunch hour, while pretending to do the crossword in the staffroom.

> "Love knot deep and stars so bright,
> Keep our union from others sight.
> Of our passion let no one tell,
> Send the Nix back down her well.
> So Mote It Be!"

I had breathed a sigh of relief as I patted the earth down firmly. It was as if a part of my turmoil had been laid to rest. I knew though that the real work had to be done at the Summer Solstice to come.

Michael came in from work looking very preoccupied, he kissed me absently as I handed him a glass of white wine.

"I had a word with Alex yesterday morning about my hours and he is going to see what he can do. He knows I've been putting in way above what I need to, so I can't see that it's going to be a problem. In fact I've arranged to go for a drink with him soon, just to tie up some loose ends."

"Oh I see." I said taking a very large gulp of wine. "Would that be Alex you're going for a drink with or Jenny?" He looked at me stunned for a moment. "Did you think that I wouldn't mention it Michael? That I would be happy to sweep it under the carpet and we could carry on pretending to patch up our marriage?" He took his mobile phone out of his pocket.

"I'm sorry that you had to find out this way," he gestured at his mobile phone. "She knows that you've found out. I told her today that it was all over."

"Michael, she is still your secretary and you have to work with her day-in, day-out. How can I ever rest easy again knowing that you are with her everyday?" I was starting to raise my voice and get upset and Michael was giving me a what-if-the-neighbours-hear kind of expression.

"We have to talk this over; work out a solution. Maybe she can be transferred to someone else's patch and I can be assigned a different secretary. I don't know, I'm just thinking aloud, but there must be a way round this, so that we can get on with our lives again."

"Do you love her?"

"No of course not, I've always loved you Jessa. You know we've been having our problems though, Jenny was just a…"

"Don't say her name please!"

"Sorry, she was just a release, a bit of fun. Someone to listen to another misunderstood husband, I suppose. I'm a cliché, okay?"

"You weren't ever going to own up to it were you? I mean if I had never found out would you have carried on the pretence of putting our marriage back together?"

"I don't know? Like I said it was lust; it had a shelf life. It would have run out of steam eventually and I suppose I thought that I could get away with it."

"Well it's not okay. None of it is okay!" I stormed into the kitchen and stood sobbing at the sink. I knew that I was not being quite fair to

Michael. Not now that we were even. Really I should just forget it and try to get on with healing our marriage. It seemed that we still had some sort of love for one another and maybe that would be enough? Michael had crossed a line that I hadn't, he had made it real with Jenny and with Laurie and me, it would never be quite real, I had made sure of that. But if I admitted the truth to myself, it was very real; just not Michael's version of real. I heard him come into the kitchen and stand behind me, tentative.

"Will I ever be forgiven?" he whispered, as if he didn't dare to ask the question. I turned around to face him and he wiped away my tears.

"I have to forgive you because I still want to be with you. I still want to make this work. I do love you, I don't know quite how, but I want to love you properly again." He pulled me closer to him.

"I'm going to take you away Jessa. Let's go on holiday, we have to save our marriage once and for all."

"We haven't been away since we first married, when we went to Italy. I think that's a great idea, no distractions, just us."

"We'll go for a whole month. Where do you want to go, it's your choice?"

"I don't know, just somewhere by the sea. I long to be by the sea, I would like to be on the sand and see the waves every single day."

"Why don't you get some brochures from the travel agent tomorrow and see what you fancy?" I nodded and there was a pause, a contemplative interlude and then he kissed me impulsively; a deep comforting kiss and I felt that I had come home.

"We're going to be alright you know, I'm going to make sure of that," he whispered, running his fingers delectably through the length of my hair.

* * *

As the week passed it felt as if something I had not expected to alter had changed. I had no more astral encounters with Laurie and I felt peacefulness resting within my heart. Michael and I were seeing more of one another and once I even met him from work to go out for a drink together in the evening, something that had never happened before. *However, my story does not end here, for the faeries you know, do not like untidiness.* There in the six week magical aperture between Beltaine and the Summer Solstice that was almost upon me was a ritual that still needed to be ridden out.

The evening of the Solstice, Michael was actually home from work before me. He had managed to get away early so that he could help me finish packing for our trip the next day.

"Are you all ready? I saw your case was packed in the bedroom," he asked as we finished a glass of wine together.

"I finished it all this morning before I went to work. I had to really because I'm going out later with the Faerie Ring. It's the Summer Solstice today."

"I know they were talking about it on the radio on the way home, the druids at Stonehenge and all that. I did wonder if you would be going out."

I had taken a bath in preparation, adding herbs in a muslin bag to concentrate my mind for the night ahead. As I was fastening my cloak I heard a car sound its horn outside. The day was just beginning to close into dusk as I peered out of the bedroom window and saw Ned's car waiting for me in the road. I thundered down the staircase and met Ned standing on my doorstep, just about to knock on the door.

"Ah, you beat me to it," he said smiling and kissing me on the cheek.

"This is my favourite night of the year, there's so much magic in the air. I just like to think of all the thousands of pagans who will be out celebrating tonight and it makes me feel tingly."

"I'm looking forward to it." We picked up Velvet on the way and we all passed the short journey talking excitedly about the night to come. By the time we reached the Magic Place, the day had almost totally succumbed to the Solstice night.

"Kel and Katri are already there by the looks of things, I can see candles flickering through the trees," Ned whispered.

"What about Laurie, how's he getting here?" I asked.

"I don't know I haven't spoken to him since the last time we all met."

"Laurie got here by train in the end." We both looked behind us as Laurie stood in the darkness of the woods. "It's a long walk from the station; I think I'll need a good drink before we start."

"I could have given you a lift if you'd rung me." said Ned.

"I didn't think, anyway I've been sitting at a desk all day, it cleared the cobwebs away."

He kissed us both and as we all walked into the clearing of the Magic Place, a panicked thought shot through my head. *What if by banishing the Nix from my inner life, I had also banished Laurie from my magical life too?* After all, the two of them had always gone hand in hand with me. Almost as soon as Laurie and I had discovered that we could meet astrally, the Nix was there too. I was not ready to be unbound from Laurie, he existed for me importantly, on a spiritual level and I needed that in my life. I could do without the ceaseless yearning for him and feeling that I only existed to be with him, but that had passed now and thus I could banish the Nix. *What if she took away that access to Laurie on the astral?* I took a deep breath and knew that the only way forward for me then was one without the Nix. She had brought me an extreme experience and through knowing that extreme I had grown. There was only one way forward, and whatever the consequences of my magical actions would be, I would have to accept them.

Kel gave me a kiss and a warm hug. "It's so good to see you Jessa, I've been looking forward to our Solstice. Is everything alright, you're looking anxious?"

"I'm all right really. I'm just glad to be here tonight, I need this ritual for lots of reasons."

"I think we all do, we have a lot of work to do in the ritual tonight. Well Katri has prepared the circle, we just need to gather ourselves together and we can begin."

Velvet, Ned, Laurie and I disappeared into the trees together. For a few moments it was simply Kelsey and Katri alone in the circle of trees; the centre of the Magic Place. As they stood in the centre I remembered last week's ritual with Queen Mab there in the sacred space with the *drawing down of the* moon, with Laurie. The Magic Place seemed charged with energy and memories for me as I stood with my friends looking at our Priest and Priestess of Elphame. They took one another's hands and closed their eyes, stood in silence together for a few moments drinking in their quiet energy and finding the centre within themselves.

"Are you ready?" I heard Katri whisper to him. Kelsey opened his eyes and nodded and then they kissed on the lips both saying, *'Blessed Be'.* Laurie and I knew that as our sign to begin, for it was the turn of the King and Queen of Cobwebs to admit the Ring. We sent Velvet and Ned into the circle and Kel and Katri welcomed them both with a kiss and *'Blessed Be'.* Laurie looked withdrawn and deep in thought. He did smile when I kissed him, as he was next entering the circle, but he was somewhere deep within himself that I could not reach. Lastly I entered the circle, carrying the faerie besom that was decorated with silver ribbons and little bells, leaning it on the tree stump altar, I came to the centre of the circle to join The Faerie Ring of Queen Mab. We all stood in the circle of perfect silence, holding hands to create the ring. The atmosphere was prickling with excitement.

We opened our chakras to begin the unfolding of melding ourselves to the place between the worlds. I felt a thrill of trepidation, but also excitement as I opened my eyes and looked at my fellow faerie seekers, all smiling. Katri had nodded to me and I collected the besom from the altar and began the ritual by sweeping the circle. I felt the energy lift and shift with each deliberate sweep of the broom; the place between the worlds was waiting for us. Kel and Katri then consecrated the circle and cast with wand, and then Laurie called the elemental quarters. There was a lot of power present and it was becoming so enveloping that it was developing into a blow-your-head-off kind of energy. Katri spoke the words of invocation in her clear Scandinavian accent to begin our circle:

> "Queen of Elfland, in your place between,
> This world of ours is quite unseen.
> With your fey King behind the shroud,
> Wave your wand and part the cloud.
> Let us meet you in this circle fey,
> An elfin journey we'll tread today.
> Blessed be."

Then we held hands once more and raised the power in a whirling dance, by chanting our favourite words from the Peter Pan novel, '*I do believe in faeries, I do, I do…*' The words spun around us all, becoming more than the words themselves, our voices spinning the words as if it were some kind of spell. '*I do believe in faeries, I do, I do…*' The great folds of material from our cloaks, robes and dresses flapped and swirled as we danced the circle, getting faster and faster as we chanted, '*I do believe in faeries; I do, I do…*' As well as our dancing bodies reeling together to raise the power, our emotions were fusing and becoming evident on our faces. It was as if we were dancing into our real selves, and the magical state would not tolerate the everyday masks, that we kept for our mundane lives. We had danced ourselves into the other realm as we suddenly reached the climax of the chant. We stood still, all breathless, holding our arms outstretched, hands clasped upwards and our eyes tightly closed. We giggled between gasping breaths of Solstice air and riding upon the effervescent energy that we had raised. I cannot tell how long we stood there, bathing in the atmosphere of magic. I felt light-headed and immersed in the ritual; nothing else mattered now that I was there among faeriewitches. The energy within the circle deepened and by now we had left reality far behind.

We sat down on the springy woodland floor with our knees touching one another to meditate. As I had closed my eyes along with everyone else I immediately felt that Laurie was calling, even summoning the wraith of me. Expecting to see Laurie before my closed eyes I saw him only for a fleeting moment, for he flickered and faded and in his place, filling my entire senses, was a larger than life nix. She was hauntingly naked, her thigh length dark hair, dripping with glittering water. Her weed coloured slanting faerie-eyes penetrated into my own and as I looked into hers I sensed the nature of reality shift. I was suddenly tossed within the in-between dimension and the air became as thick as treacle, so thick that I fancy I could hear it glooping past my ears.

She had offered her tapered hand and this time I took it, the moment I did, my whole body shuddered with the effect she had upon my entire being. All at once I became naked like her, as we held hands and my skin was covered in water. I was aware of the presence of every single droplet of water upon my body, as if I was experiencing a heightened sense of perception. This increased awareness was an acute sensual pleasure and as every droplet ran slowly down my skin, it was the most erotic experience that I had ever encountered. It was as if each droplet was a tiny finger caressing my bare skin. For a few moments I could only sit and breathe deeply with pleasure, as if the water was strangely making love to me. Then the enchanting Nix cupped my face in her hands and kissed me, the most rousing and carnal act I will ever know. That kiss alone brought me to a tumultuous orgasm, as if waves lapped over me like the waves of the sea, kissing every inch of my skin.

By now the others were deep in meditation and did not seem to notice my pleasure wrapped in darkness. Only Laurie stared deeply into me as I opened my eyes and he looked how I felt. I suddenly realised that he had just gone through the very same experience with the Nix. This had been her way of saying farewell to us both. With her kiss I knew that she had gone down her well forever. Now she had left her exquisite mark on both of us.

Laurie had looked in shock in the wake of the Nix and I felt a massive surge of love for him and a sense of relief swept over me. She had gone, it was all over and we were liberated from the nympholeptic desire. The Nix's water had acted as a living mirror to me and I could now see my life clearly. The Nix had chosen me, or was it me that had chosen her; to show me myself and set me free.

* * *

Picture us all now in the Wharton's Victorian walled garden on this Solstice night. The enchanted apple tree has hung from its boughs thirteen candle lanterns swaying magically in the light breeze. Now is the time of the Midsummer Feast and even though it is gone midnight, we are all seated on a rug beneath the luminary lantern light of the apple tree. Before us is Ned's delightful home-baked spread. There are cheese and onion scones, hunks of French bread with nettle soup, home-brewed elderflower champagne with double-chocolate chip cookies and raspberry ice cream. "A toast to Midsummer Night and the Faerie Ring of Queen Mab," hailed Kelsey holding up his glass of elderflower champagne.

"And to Ned's delumptious cooking!" said Velvet, raising her glass in unison. Everyone made noises of approval, especially Ned and clinked glasses together saying, '*Blessed be*', as we did so. There was a glorious relaxed feeling that all energy had been spent and we could all float on the restful lull that now ensued. It still felt as if we were in faerie time as we celebrated our Solstice ritual in the timeless bewitching garden of lanterns. There was much giggling and frivolity by this time as not only had a lot of alcohol been consumed but Ned had plaited Velvet's long creamy hair without her knowing and had knotted it to a low branch of the apple tree. When she attempted to get up to fill her glass, she found herself attached to the tree.

Kelsey put on some quaint music from the 1920's. He held his hand out for Katri to take and she did so, standing up and smiling. "May I have the pleasure of this dance?" he asked grinning. Katri nodded and he whisked her around the garden. Ned quickly took Kel's lead and also held out his hand for Velvet, who was by now unattached from the tree.

"Madam, may I have the pleasure?" he asked theatrically.

"Darling, the pleasure is all mine," she purred equally dramatically.

Laurie and I sat together watching the two couples dancing and I felt as if I belonged to a faerie ball. Kelsey had on a moss green plaid kilt which he had worn for the ritual and Katri danced elegantly in her long mediaeval style dress. She wore a sparkling tiara of quartz and amethyst crystals in her black hair and her shoes sparkled with beads of the same stones.

Ned wore a robe of black velvet and a crown of woven ivy leaves upon his head, and he looked at Velvet with a definite sparkle in his eye. This had been Velvet's first ritual with the Faerie Ring, as we felt that she was more than ready. See her now dancing with Ned, knowing that she is held in the timeless place of faerie, for just one night that feels it is without end. She is wearing a faun layered floaty dress with an enormous pair of hand-made gauzy faerie wings attached to her back. She wears a crown of ox-eye daisies in her hair and to me she looks like a faerie princess.

Laurie and I exchanged glances and he put his hand over mine, squeezing it warmly. "I'm still in shock over the Nix, aren't you?" he whispered and I nodded.

"I never expected... it was so intense. In fact if a nix hangover exists, I have one."

"Do you think she's gone for good? It felt absolute, as if it was her big finale."

"Yes, she's gone. I have something to admit, I did do a banishing spell for her last week because I knew that if she wasn't in my life anymore things would feel more in control, more normal once again."

"You know then that this has to end, don't you, for now anyway Jessa? You'll always be my Faerie Priestess whatever, you know that."

"And you my Faerie Priest. Perhaps this was just the way it had to begin, our elfin initiation into the role of the cobwebbed King and Queen."

"Yes, this is just the beginning; it feels better when you say it that way." He stood up and held out his hand to me and I smiled and took it. "Join me in this dance, won't you?" he asked and I stood up as he put his hand upon my waist and we joined the other giggling couples within the Midsummer dancing.

"I'm going away for a while Jessa, I'm sorry," he whispered and for a moment I looked at him stunned.

"I think that you are being removed from my life. We have to both get back on track, its okay."

"It's only for six months, but it's a great opportunity and I don't want to pass it up. There's an archaeology project on the Isle of Lewis. Where I am now as a council archaeologist, it's so tied up with red tape, I would just like to get my teeth into something exciting for a breath of fresh air. Jane is coming with me and she's arranged to work from home for that time. It's finite, so she can do it for a while."

"It sounds very exciting, I'm happy for you Laurie, truly I am." He looked relieved at my reaction. "I am going away too, not for as long as you. Michael and I are going to Venice for a month beginning tomorrow. We've got a lot of making up to do. I felt I needed to be by the sea, to feel free…" Laurie looked shocked all of a sudden and his expression changed.

"What's the matter Laurie?" He stopped our dancing and rested his forehead upon my shoulder and sighed deeply.

"Jessamyn," he whispered into my right ear, so softly that it sounded like a magical spell. "Do you remember when we both met Queen Mab in the meadow that night and you told me the rhyme to enter Faerie Land?"

"I remember the night of course, but not the verse, it has eluded me. I so wish that I could remember it." He looked into my eyes and our faces were so close that our noses were almost touching and his grip on me had tightened.

"Be careful what you wish for Jessa." He began to dance with me again as Kel and Katri swirled past us, giggling.

"What do you mean?" I whispered.

"I mean that Jessa, *I* have always remembered the rhyme. You never thought to ask me did you?"

"I always assumed that you had forgotten it too. So why haven't you told me; why have you left it until now?"

"Because I knew there would be a moment and that moment is now." We both instinctively stopped dancing and we stood in the middle of the lawn as if no one else existed, it was only Laurie and I in those moments. I knew they were the last moments we would spend together like this; the last droplet of the Nix's spell. Then he whispered the words, the verse of my ending and my beginning and it felt as if we were in a place suspended like a glass ball hanging from a tree. The words of the rhyme seemed to last forever and his whispering voice was like a bewitching charm upon me. I knew now that I had learnt that love needed never to be exclusive, but commitment was. When he had finished I still felt under the spell of the rhyme and he broke it by kissing me gently on the cheek.

"Will you write it down for me?" I asked numbly, he nodded and our spell was then forever broken. We joined the dance of the Midsummer Solstice at our little lantern lit faerie ball. I knew that on this Solstice night; all was well and everything had been and was as it should be.

Epilogue

Expect Magic … and it will happen

'And then from her charméd eye release
…and all things shall be peace.'

William Shakespeare, A Midsummer Night's Dream

When I reached home after the Solstice festivities it was dawn and the birds were singing their morning chorus. I checked that everything was packed and ready for us to go away in a few hours time. Before I sank into bed next to Michael I took the verse out of my felt handbag. Reading Queen Mab's verse once again, I knew that I remembered it well. It was another lost knowing from the fey, that I would also never forget.

> *Now that you are gone I can say I love you*
> *Your life will go on and you will forget…*
> *And I will remember you at the side of the sea.*
> *You that never knew how much I loved you*
> *Maybe in another's arms you will manage to forget…*
> *Maybe you will look at another, the same way you looked*
> *at me on that day*
> *And I will remember you at the side of the sea…*

As I said, there are some things that are broken if one speaks of them, so you won't tell anyone will you? I am trusting you with my faerie secret.

Also by Alicen Geddes-Ward

Faeriecraft,

Few people have had direct contact with the Faerie world, but Alicen Geddes-Ward is one of them. Acknowledged as one of the UK's leading experts on the Faerie realms, Alicen has created a book that will allow other people to deepen their connection with Faeries. In this book she describes her powerful encounters with the Faeries who have stepped forward to teach and guide her. Using practical techniques such as meditation, ceremony and visualization this is a powerful introductory guide for anyone interested in Faeries or Wiccan topics.

Hay House, London, 2005. Co-authored and illustrated by Neil Geddes-Ward, (Non-fiction) ISBN 1401905579

Music and Meditation CDs

Sleeve notes for Llewellyn and Juliana, *Journey to the Faeries,* New World Music, 2003

Sleeve notes for Llewellyn and Juliana, *Faerie Lore, Journey to the Faerie Ring,* Paradise Music, publication date 2006

The Faerie Cottage: Guided Meditation for Relaxation and Imagination, featuring music by Llewellyn, New World Music, publication date 2004

Journey to the Faerie Ring, Guided Meditations, featuring music by Llewellyn, Paradise Music, publication date 2006

Faerie Workshop, Guided Meditations, featuring music by Llewellyn, Paradise Music, publication date 2006

Also published by Winged Feet Productions

The Hidden Masters and the Unspeakable Evil
by Jack Barrow

Clint, Nigel and Wayne are three middle aged friends with a secret. They are master magicians, Hidden Masters in fact. However, they are not Hidden Tibetan Masters for they are The Three Hidden Masters, two from Hemel Hempstead and one from Bricket Wood. They discover a conspiracy to build casinos in Blackpool, thus making it the Las Vegas of the north, turning the resort into a seedy tacky and depraved town. Something needs to be done. Unable to turn down a challenge they head north at the weekend to put an end to the plot. However, they need to save the universe by Sunday evening because they have to be back at work on Monday morning. This is occult fiction where magick and supernatural events occur in the modern world, but this book is not for kids; this is magickal fiction strictly for adults. What you will find is tarot, astrology and grown men in robes, performing rituals, and generally behaving strangely. All this is wrapped up in Jack Barrow's off-beat wit and quirky perspective on the counter culture of modern occult paganism, pop philosophy, cheap dark rum and drugs.

Publication date 2006, (fiction) ISBN 0-9515329-1-X

Satanic Viruses: The Fall of the Roman Empire and How to Bring it About by Jack Barrow

Latest edition of Jack Barrow's observations on the changes in the world as we move into the Age of Aquarius. Originally published in 1989 and now in its third edition this book uses astrology, tarot, philosophy, politics and more to examine the nature of the times in which we live.

- Was September 11th a manifestation of the changes that will bring Crowley's New Aeon?
- Has time run out for the established religions of the world?
- Just when did science go loony?
- Was the fall of the Berlin Wall the first major evidence that Armageddon is really underway, and that it won't all be bad?
- Is girl power just one example of the emergence of Crowley's scarlet woman, Spare's primitive woman and Dion Fortune's priestly woman of power?
- Does the existence of international terrorism indicate that the modern scientific paradigm has reached its limits?
- Is the future of humanity dependent or our ability to steer tiny little boats?
- Can YOU change the world with photocopies or spam?

Publication date 2007, (non fiction) ISBN 987-0-9515329-3-5